INFIDEL

PROTECTORS
UNDERCOVER
—TEAM ONE—

BOOK FOUR

USA TODAY BESTSELLING AUTHOR

HEATHER SLADE

UNDERCOVER INFIDEL
Copyright © 2024

This book is a work of fiction. All names, characters, locations, and incidents are products of the authors' imaginations. Any resemblance to actual persons, things, living or dead, locales, or events is entirely coincidental.

979-8-88649-614-7

MORE FROM AUTHOR HEATHER SLADE

BUTLER RANCH
Kade's Worth
Brodie's Promise
Maddox's Truce
Naughton's Secret
Mercer's Vow
Kade's Return
Butler Ranch Christmas

WICKED WINEMAKERS
FIRST LABEL
Brix's Bid
Ridge's Release
Press' Passion
Zin's Sins
Tryst's Temptation

WICKED WINEMAKERS
SECOND LABEL
Beau's Beloved
Cru's Crush
Bit's Bliss
Snapper's Seduction
Kick's Kiss

ROARING FORK RANCH
Roaring Fork Wrangler
Roaring Fork Roughstock
Roaring Fork Rockstar
Roaring Fork Rooker
Roaring Fork Bridger

PROTECTORS
UNDERCOVER TEAM ONE
Undercover Agent
Undercover Emissary
Undercover Savior
Undercover Infidel
Undercover Shadow

PROTECTORS
UNDERCOVER TEAM TWO
Undercover Renegade
Undercover Archon
Undercover Rogue
Undercover Vanguard
Undercover Paragon

K19 GENESIS COALITION
Code Name: Sundance
Code Name: Rawhide
Code Name: Dallas
Code Name: Wraith
Code Name: Preacher

K19 SECURITY
SOLUTIONS TEAM ONE
Razor's Edge
Gunner's Redemption
Mistletoe's Magic
Mantis' Desire
Dutch's Salvation

K19 SECURITY
SOLUTIONS TEAM TWO
Striker's Choice
Monk's Fire
Halo's Oath
Tackle's Honor
Onyx's Awakening

K19 SHADOW OPERATIONS
TEAM ONE
Code Name: Ranger
Code Name: Diesel
Code Name: Wasp
Code Name: Cowboy
Code Name: Mayhem

K19 ALLIED INTELLIGENCE
TEAM ONE
Code Name: Ares
Code Name: Cayman
Code Name: Poseidon
Code Name: Zeppelin
Code Name: Magnet

K19 ALLIED INTELLIGENCE
TEAM TWO
Code Name: Puck
Code Name: Michelangelo
Code Name: Typhon
Code Name: Hornet
Code Name: Reaper

New series coming soon:
MINERVA PROTOCOL
Code Name: Blackjack
Code Name: Dagger
Code Name: Nexus
Code Name: Ember
Code Name: Nomad

K19 SENTINEL CYBER
TEAM ONE
Code Name: Admiral
Code Name: Dante
Code Name: Grit
Code Name: Tank
Code Name: Atticus

K19 SENTINEL CYBER
TEAM TWO
Code Name: Admiral
Code Name: Dante
Code Name: Grit
Code Name: Tank
Code Name: Atticus

THE ROYAL AGENTS
OF MI6
Make Me Shiver
Drive Me Wilder
Feel My Pinch
Chase My Shadow
Find My Angel

THE INVINCIBLES
TEAM ONE
Code Name: Deck
Code Name: Edge
Code Name: Grinder
Code Name: Rile
Code Name: Smoke

THE INVINCIBLES
TEAM TWO
Code Name: Buck
Code Name: Irish
Code Name: Saint
Code Name: Hammer
Code Name: Rip

THE UNSTOPPABLES
TEAM ONE
Code Name: Fury
Code Name: Merried
Code Name: Vex
Code Name: Steel
Code Name: Jagger

COWBOYS OF
CRESTED BUTTE
A Cowboy Falls
A Cowboy's Dance
A Cowboy's Kiss
A Cowboy Stays
A Cowboy Wins

Table of Contents

1

Con

The amber liquid in my glass caught the moonlight streaming in through the floor-to-ceiling windows of my private office at Blackmoor Castle. Zero three hundred was a wretched hour to be awake, yet every night for the past week, my eyes had sprung open at the same time with the same question—how did I miss that a woman I'd pursued romantically was actually the mastermind behind the most lethal weapons system since the atomic bomb?

That her body now lay on a cold slab in the SIS morgue did nothing to assuage the terror behind my insomnia. She hadn't been working alone, and we had no leads on her accomplices. The intel we'd gathered suggested Tower-Meridian's vast shipping infrastructure remained operational despite her death, which raised disturbing questions.

If Fallon had been using the company's global network for her schemes, who was controlling it now? And what were they using it for? The company that had seemed merely suspicious in Sullivan's initial investigation could now be the vehicle for something far worse.

I'd taken to using the sleepless hours when such thoughts drove me to a maddening level of frustration to exhaust myself physically. Tonight proved no different. After a ten-mile run on the treadmill in my gym, I was more wired than tired, so rather than attempt to sleep again, I returned to what I referred to as my operations hub.

It was located in the underground level of my home's east wing and was where I balanced my discreet information brokerage with the legitimate data-protection business that provided its cover.

I removed my sweat-soaked shirt and studied the endless stream of feeds on multiple monitors, pacing between them since my constant state of anxiety kept me from sitting for more than a few minutes at a time.

I poured another scotch, knowing it would only worsen my insomnia. After yesterday, I needed it. I couldn't fathom that, once again, I'd be working with someone who infuriated me even as her presence affected me in ways I'd vowed a woman never would again.

Being teamed with Dr. Margot Sterling, MI6's expert on cognitive warfare systems, felt like punishment, mainly because I had to concede—albeit only to myself—that she was damned good at her job. There were times when I'd go so far as to think she might be almost as good as I was.

I finished my drink and was headed back to the gym to do a second workout when a flash of red caught my eye.

"Bloody hell," I growled when I noticed someone bypass my digital safeguards.

Instead of shutting them out, I watched in fascination as they navigated my defenses with unexpected ease, anticipating my countermoves before I made them.

On a hunch that the perpetrator wanted me to know who they were, I traced the intrusion, unsurprised to find it came from the facility I knew housed MI6's AI-research division.

With a few keystrokes, I pulled up the CCTV feeds through the sophisticated systems that made my operations hub the envy of both government agencies and private security firms. The building appeared empty except for one illuminated office, where I could make out a woman with long dark hair and confident posture. Just as I'd sensed who my hacker was, she knew I was watching.

Within seconds, every one of my screens but one went black. On the remaining monitor, the CCTV footage cleared and text appeared, letter by letter.

While almost as impressive as you are, your code contains a critical vulnerability, Lord Blackmoor.

The message disappeared, and briefly, a woman's face appeared. She looked directly into the camera with a knowing smirk that quickened my pulse. Then she vanished, replaced by another message.

Your office at Blackmoor. 0900. And, Con? Do have a shirt on when I arrive.

When my systems restored as if nothing had happened, I poured myself another scotch and raised it to the screen in acknowledgment. Whether she could see me do it or not filled me with unfamiliar foreboding.

While no system was infallible, no one had gotten as deep as she had. Breach countermeasures existed for people just like her.

In Dr. Sterling's case, her formidable intellect would either rattle my already faltering confidence or she would prove to be my most worthy opponent. Either way, tomorrow would be interesting.

The whiskey was a mistake. The throbbing behind my eyes confirmed it as I stood beneath the shower at zero seven hundred. Three hours of sleep couldn't remedy the combination of alcohol and exhaustion.

I pressed my palms against the marble tile, letting the water pound my neck as I mentally retraced every line of code I'd written. Her intrusion shouldn't have been possible. I'd believed every firewall and fail-safe was impenetrable. I'd designed them myself. Clearly, I was wrong.

She'd found a way. That "critical vulnerability" she'd mentioned haunted me more than the memories of Fallon Wallace.

Fallon. Chimera. The name twisted something inside me. I had been the quintessential fool to her duplicity. My expertise in reading people had failed completely. It was a humiliation I couldn't tolerate repeating.

Yet now, another brilliant woman was challenging me directly. I couldn't decide if Dr. Sterling's boldness was refreshing or reckless.

Both, I decided as I shut off the water.

By zero eight thirty, I was at my desk in my study in Blackmoor's east wing, dressed in a custom navy suit with no tie. I'd chosen this location rather than my operations hub, where I allowed no one entry other than upper-level staff. It was still equipped with impressive technology, but not my most sensitive equipment. I wasn't about to give Dr. Sterling access to everything after her stunt.

The gate cam showed a car approaching at zero eight forty-five. Fifteen minutes early. A calculated move to catch me unprepared.

"Nicely played, Dr. Sterling," I acknowledged, watching her interaction with my gate staff.

Her dark hair was pulled back in a sleek knot, and she wore a tailored charcoal suit over a crimson silk blouse that reminded me of the warning flashes on my screen last night.

Once inside, her heels resonated against the marble, each step deliberate as she followed my head of security through the main hall.

Rather than wait for her to be announced, I opened the door just as they approached.

"I'll take it from here. Thank you, Bastion." Daniel Fraser, who referred to himself as my "defense chief," also served in an almost undercover capacity as my butler. The man was a former Royal Marine who'd been with me for several years.

I stepped aside to let her enter and noticed her perfume—subtle and expensive.

"Dr. Sterling," I said, closing the door. "Most people request a meeting rather than hacking their way into one."

She turned, taking in my study with one sweeping glance before meeting my eyes. "Most people aren't dealing with the aftermath of Chimera's betrayal and a weapons system that could redefine warfare as we know it."

Her voice was lower than I remembered, with a hint of an accent I couldn't place.

"And you thought hacking into my system would what—impress me?" I moved to the window, giving her my profile rather than my full attention.

"No." Her simple utterance made me turn around. "I thought it would prove I'm not just another analyst you can dismiss or manipulate. I needed to establish certain ground rules before Typhon forces us to work together."

Typhon—my commander at Unit 23 and the bastard who'd agreed to this arrangement with Sterling's boss, Viper, the new MI6 chief.

"You've succeeded in proving you have technical skills," I conceded. "Though to be fair, I hadn't yet patched the breach point you exploited. An oversight I've since corrected."

Her lips curved slightly. "Have you?"

The question hung between us, a challenge that stirred something in my chest. This woman wasn't intimidated by my reputation or my title. The realization was oddly exhilarating.

"What exactly does Viper expect us to accomplish together?" I asked, moving to the bar cart near my desk. "Coffee?"

"Tea, please." She took a seat without waiting for an invitation, crossing her legs. "She and Typhon want us to track down the network behind Chimera's AI-weapons program, aka Project Labyrinth."

I handed her a cup and took my own seat. "I'm already doing that."

"Without access to MI6's resources? Without specialized knowledge of neural networks and militarized AI architecture?" She took a sip, watching me over the rim of her cup. "You're good, Lord Blackmoor—"

"Con."

"Con," she amended. "As I said, you're good. But this is my field of expertise."

Before I could respond, my private mobile buzzed.

"Excuse me." I stood and moved away from the table. "Tag. What is it?"

"Nightingale's been extracted from Syria," he began. "They're debriefing her at Station G now, and what we're hearing goes beyond what was contained in the encrypted file she sent. Her background in cryptanalysis has enabled her to intercept communications tied to Labyrinth that others missed."

Station G, our field office in Glasgow, was housed in a converted warehouse near the River Clyde. Established specifically for operations in western Scotland, it saved us the journey to either Edinburgh or Vauxhall Cross when time mattered.

Leila Nassar, code name Nightingale, was a highly skilled Unit 23 field operative. That Tag, who was one of my closest friends and a respected colleague, would reach out about the information she was providing in the debrief was promising.

"I'll be there in an hour," I told him, ending the call. After calculating the flight time in my private helicopter—thirty minutes versus a two-hour drive—I sent a message to my pilot, asking him to meet us at the helipad.

"Problem?" Dr. Sterling asked.

"Opportunity. One of our operatives has returned from Syria with information that may be relevant to Project Labyrinth."

"I'm coming with you."

It wasn't a request, and surprisingly, I didn't want to refuse. Whatever tension sparked between us—personal or professional—the mission took precedence.

"Fair warning," I said as I collected my mobile and a slim leather portfolio. "Once we step out that door, we're allies, Dr. Sterling. I expect the same level of transparency from you that you're demanding from me."

She approached until we stood nearly toe-to-toe, close enough for me to see flecks of gold in her dark eyes.

"Call me Lex," she said. I couldn't recall her actual code name as the shortened version was often chosen for brevity for someone working on complex AI systems. The full meaning sometimes became less important than the level of capability required. "And I should warn you—I only infiltrate systems I respect."

The subtext wasn't lost on me. I opened the door and gestured for her to precede me.

"After you, Lex."

As we walked to the helipad, two things rose to the forefront of my mind. First, whatever those behind Project Labyrinth were planning would prove to be more deadly than any of us suspected. And second, working with Dr. Margot Sterling would be the greatest challenge—and possibly the greatest temptation—I had ever faced.

2

Lex

Lord Blackmoor's helicopter sliced through the morning sky, the sleek black machine as arrogant as its owner. Below us, the Scottish countryside unfurled like a patchwork quilt, mist still clinging to the glens and valleys as the sun crept higher.

I studied Con Carnegie from the corner of my eye, noting the tight line of his jaw and the focused intensity of his gaze as he stared out the window. The rays filtered by clouds caught the angles of his face, highlighting cheekbones that could cut glass and the dark stubble that only enhanced his rugged charm.

Not that I was paying attention to his appeal. I was professionally assessing a colleague. Nothing more.

"You're staring, Dr. Sterling," he said without turning his head.

"I was wondering if you'd yet realized your system's second vulnerability," I replied smoothly.

A muscle in his jaw twitched. Point to me.

"Three, in fact. None of which you could have exploited in the manner you did," Con growled.

"Perhaps you're not looking in the right places."

He turned then, his blue eyes meeting mine with an intensity that sent an unwelcome warmth up my spine. "Or perhaps you had inside help."

I laughed, genuinely amused. "Your ego won't allow for the possibility that someone might simply be better than you?"

He didn't smile, but something akin to respect flashed in his expression. "Few people are."

"Well," I said, crossing my legs and brushing an imaginary piece of lint from my trousers. "I'm not most people."

A smirk played at the corners of his mouth. "That much is painfully obvious."

The pilot's voice came through our headsets, announcing our descent into Glasgow, interrupting our banter. Con looked away, the brief moment of connection severed as he returned to business mode.

It was an important reminder for me to do the same. With the unexpected retirement of my boss and mentor, Dr. McLaren, just weeks ago, the pressure to prove myself as MI6's foremost AI expert fell squarely on my shoulders. I wouldn't let anyone—especially not the infamous Infidel—see any hint of insecurity. My parents had raised me to stand on my own before their untimely deaths, and I'd honor their memory by being unshakable now, when it mattered most.

"Tell me more about the situation with Nightingale," I said.

"As you're aware, the rebel forces in Syria took control of the government in a coup that resulted in the country's president fleeing to Russia."

"Go on."

"According to the secure message she sent Tag, Nightingale has reason to believe her cover was blown and, thus, sent an agent-in-peril alert to both Unit 23 and her team on the ground. Her extraction was successful, and she's being debriefed at our field office in Glasgow."

"You said there's reason to believe she has evidence relevant to Project Labyrinth. Relating specifically to Chimera?"

"According to Tag, yes. Nightingale has been embedded in Damascus for nearly two years. Her most recent op was tracking Fallon Wallace's contacts."

The network of dangerous connections the deceased woman was believed to have were critical threads for us to follow.

"If she's been able to identify who's continuing Wallace's work, that could be a significant lead. Although I doubt it would be that simple."

Con inclined his head in agreement.

The helicopter touched down on a landing pad near the river. A nondescript, gray building loomed before us, its windows tinted to opacity. As the rotors slowed, Niall MacTaggert strode toward us, his features set in grim lines. The Earl of Glenshadow—code name Obsidian, though I knew his friends called him Tag—moved with the deadly grace I remembered from our first meeting.

"About bloody time," he said, his accent heavier than I'd previously noticed. He turned to me. "Apologies. Good to see you again, Lex. We can certainly use your expertise."

"Good to see you again too," I replied. "However, the consensus appears to be that I'm second best," I added with a pointed look at Con. "But I'll do."

Tag let out a short bark of laughter. "Oh, she'll fit right in." He sobered quickly.

"Brief us on the way," Con said as we followed Tag toward an unmarked side entrance.

"As she's a Unit-23 asset, only Typhon has full clearance for what Nightingale is reporting," said Tag as we walked.

Once inside, he took us into an observation room with one-way glass, where Leviticus "Typhon" Marras waited.

"Thank you for coming," said Typhon, nodding at Con and me, then motioning to the adjacent room, where Nightingale was being interviewed. "They're currently discussing what she describes as 'integration systems.'"

"The holy grail of autonomous AI weaponry," Con commented.

"Armaments that can't be turned against its makers," I added. "I'd like to speak with her."

All three men turned to look at me.

"With respect," Tag began, "I don't think that's an appropriate ask."

"Given this is my area of expertise, there might be technical details she was privy to that could easily be misunderstood."

"Do it," Typhon said, alerting the interview team to take a break.

When I entered the room, Nightingale looked up at me, her dark eyes assessing.

"I don't know you," she said.

"Dr. Margot Sterling. I'm an MI6 AI specialist." I showed her my credentials, and when she gestured to the chair, I sat across from her. "I need to understand exactly what you heard about the integration process."

For ten minutes, I led the woman through technical questions. As she reiterated the various conversations she'd been privy to, a chilling picture emerged of exactly what I'd feared.

After signaling we were finished, I thanked her and returned to the room where the three men waited.

"There's someone I know who I believe can help. I'd like to schedule a consult," I began. "Dr. Evelyn McLaren."

"Absolutely not," Con said before the other man even opened his mouth.

I bristled. "Why not?"

"The fewer people involved in this investigation, the better."

"I completely disagree," I said, folding my arms. "As the person responsible for creating the Artificial Intelligence Ethics division for SIS fifteen years ago, she knows more about the technology than most anyone in the world."

"She's no longer with SIS," Con stated.

"That's irrelevant. Dr. McLaren mentored me. Regardless of what you're insinuating, she's beyond reproach."

"People are rarely what they seem," Con replied coolly.

My temper flared. "If you're accusing—"

"I'm *saying* we need to pick and choose who from MI6 is vetted and who isn't."

I was incredulous. "*Vetted?* Wait. You said MI6."

"That's right," Con responded, raising his chin.

I looked between him and Typhon. When I glanced over at Tag, his attention was fixated on the woman on the opposite side of the glass.

"So what you're saying is, anyone affiliated with Unit 23 is automatically vetted and those of us with MI6 need additional clearance?"

"I never said anyone would be read in automatically. What I said is we need to be mindful of how many people we trust enough to join the mission—"

"This from the man who missed all the signs that his girlfriend was developing weapons of mass destruction?" The words left my mouth before I could stop them.

The room went silent, and Con's face hardened.

"Enough." Typhon's voice was quiet but commanding. "This is precisely why I had reservations when Viper suggested this arrangement." He looked from Con to me. "Your personal feelings are irrelevant. Dr. Sterling, your expertise in AI-weapons systems is unparalleled. Infidel, your cybersecurity knowledge is equally valuable. You will work together professionally, or I will find replacements who can."

Two hours into our agreed-upon truce, Tag stayed behind with Nightingale, who we were told would continue the debrief in the morning. Typhon had returned to London, leaving Con and me to fly back to Blackmoor.

The helicopter ride was silent for fifteen minutes. I stared out the window, reviewing everything we'd learned.

"I apologize," Con said over the headset.

I turned. "For?"

"Jumping down your throat about McLaren."

"And I apologize for the comment about Fallon Wallace. It was uncalled for."

When he looked away, I studied him like I had earlier. The man was more complex than any I'd ever known, and in my professional circles, that was saying something.

As if he felt my eyes on him, he turned abruptly and caught me staring.

"Why did you really hack my system last night?" he asked quietly.

I considered deflecting, but decided on honesty. "I needed to know if you were as good as your reputation. If we're going to put a stop to Labyrinth's AI advances,

I need a partner I can rely on. Not just another aristocrat playing at espionage."

Something like respect flickered in his eyes. "And your conclusion?"

I allowed myself a small smile. "You passed."

As Blackmoor Castle came into view, I felt an unexpected sense of anticipation. Working with Conrad Carnegie would be challenging, frustrating, and possibly dangerous.

It might also be the most intellectually stimulating partnership of my career.

If we didn't kill each other first.

3

Con

The return trip to Blackmoor had been mercifully quiet. After the tension in Glasgow, I was grateful for the uninterrupted time to absorb what we'd learned from Nightingale. As we landed, the afternoon shadows stretched across the grounds, the winter sun already beginning its early descent in the Highland sky.

Lex followed me from the helipad with determined strides, her focus evident in the set of her shoulders. Neither of us spoke much since Typhon's reprimand about our professional behavior, and I found myself oddly concerned with maintaining the fragile truce we'd established.

"We should get started immediately," she said as we entered the castle through the east entrance. "The information from Nightingale won't stay current for long. The players will rapidly change tactics once they suspect exposure."

"Roger that." I gestured to Bastion as we came inside. "And every hour that passes gives the Labyrinth consortium more time to advance their project."

Rather than take her to my ops hub, I led Lex back to my study. The fire had been lit in anticipation of our return, casting a warm glow across the room's Persian rugs. Modern technology blended seamlessly with the centuries-old architecture—much like my own life, straddling two worlds.

"Still keeping me from your actual ops room, I see," Lex commented.

"For now." I moved to the sideboard where Mrs. Thorne, my head housekeeper, had left a tea service. "Would you prefer Earl Grey or something stronger?"

"The blend is fine, thank you. I need a clear head."

I poured us both a cup, watching as she explored the space, running her fingers along the spines of leather-bound books that had belonged to my father and his father before him.

"So," she said, accepting the drink I offered. "Let's establish our approach. I suggest we start by cross-referencing the evidence from Nightingale with MI6's database on known weapons developers who special-ize in AI integration."

"My network might prove more efficient," I coun-tered, taking a seat at the table where I typically worked while in here. "There are sources who won't speak to official agencies under any circumstances."

She arched a brow. "Your 'network' being the con-tacts from your shadier business interests?"

"I prefer 'alternative enterprises,'" I replied, main-taining a neutral tone despite her sarcasm. "Sources cultivated over years."

"Without accountability or any way to validate what they're saying. We need confirmed information, not whispers from profiteers who'd sell you whatever you want to hear."

"They have proved reliable in circumstances where conventional methods failed."

"And when they aren't reliable?" She set down her cup with more force than necessary. "Project Labyrinth isn't one of your business ventures, Infidel. The stakes here affect global stability."

I stood and returned to the sideboard where, rather than tea, I poured myself two fingers of scotch. "I take exception to your tone, Dr. Sterling. I'm well aware of the gravity of the situation. Perhaps to a greater extent than you are."

Her gaze landed on my glass, and she scoffed. "Then, I would think you'd understand why we need multiple ways to cross-check any information we gather."

"This conversation is not only growing tiresome…" Before I finished the thought, my secure mobile vibrated with an encrypted message. I glanced down, immediately recognizing the identifier—Kestrel, one of my less savory but consistently reliable sources.

Need to talk. Have intel on recent AI components moving through nonstandard channels. Available at 22:00 your time. Same encryption method as last time.

After raising a brow at the serendipity of the message's arrival, I texted back a quick confirmation.

"Something important?" Dr. Sterling asked, watching my face too closely for comfort.

"Just a schedule update," I replied, slipping the mobile into my pocket. "Nothing urgent."

Her expression told me she didn't believe me, but she didn't press the issue.

A knock at the door saved me from further interrogation. Bastion appeared with his usual aptitude.

"My lord, the Earl of Glenshadow has arrived and asks if you're available."

"Show him in, please."

Moments later, Tag strode through the door, his imposing frame filling the entrance. Despite his aristocratic title, there was nothing soft about Niall MacTaggert. Before his eyes landed on Lex, he swept the room with the instinctive awareness of the assassin he was.

"Dr. Sterling. Didn't expect you to still be here."

She raised her chin. "We hardly have time to waste."

"Copy that." He turned to me. "Any progress?"

"We're currently establishing parameters," I responded.

"I've got updates from Glasgow," Tag said, accepting the glass of scotch I offered. "Rather than wait until tomorrow, Nightingale's debrief concluded after you left. Typhon had her moved to a secure location."

"Was that necessary?" Lex asked.

"It was. Her cover was thoroughly blown, which meant there was already chatter about a price on her head."

"Good God," I exclaimed. "That didn't take long."

"It doesn't usually," Tag replied. "Anyway, Typhon wants us to proceed as if her intel is compromised."

"Which brings us back to our approach," Lex said, glancing from Tag to me. "We need to pursue multiple avenues simultaneously."

"Let's divide our resources," said Tag. "I'm heading to Glenshadow now, but will be available tomorrow. Which, by the way, is New Year's Eve."

"So it is," I said under my breath, remembering several that he, I, and our two closest friends—Ash and Gus—had spent together, starting when we were wee lads. Once we reached adulthood, the celebrations became fewer and farther between, given the four of us had pursued careers in espionage that took us through hell together more times than I could count. We each brought something unique to our tightly knit unit—Tag's lethal instincts, Ash's unparalleled sniper capabilities, Gus's unwavering loyalty and technical skill. They accepted my less conventional methods without judgment, even when I kept certain aspects of my operations compartmentalized.

That thought made me glance at Lex, who was listening intently to Tag's reminiscences of previous years' celebrations, told much to my dismay. There was something about her that unsettled me—not just her impressive intellect or her directness, but the way she seemed to see through the crafted layers of my persona.

"Earth to Carnegie," Tag said, breaking into my thoughts.

"Sorry, just thinking."

"I said I need to head out. Early start tomorrow." He downed the last of his scotch and stood. "Good luck with your collaboration. You'll need it." The last bit was said with a wry smile that made me want to punch him.

After Tag departed, Lex turned to me, arms crossed. "So, are you going to tell me about the message you received earlier? The one you deliberately hid from me?"

"I wasn't hiding anything," I lied automatically.

"Transparency works both ways, Lord Blackmoor." Her use of my title was intentionally formal. "You asked for it from me this morning, yet you're deliberately lying as well as concealing communications."

Her accuracy struck a nerve, and I raised a brow.

She leaned forward. "Your body language speaks volumes, Con. The way you angled the screen. The tension in your jaw when you dismissed it as nothing important."

I had two choices—continue the charade or admit she was right. I chose the latter, if only because lying would prove her point even more effectively than the truth.

"I received a message from one of my contacts. He claims to have information about AIWS movement. We're scheduled to videoconference at twenty-two hundred hours."

She appeared satisfied, yet her words proved I was wrong. "Here? Meaning in your *secondary* workspace?"

I stood, making a decision I hoped wouldn't come back to haunt me. "Come with me."

I led her through the castle to the east wing, then down to the underground level where military-grade defense systems became more evident with each step. After passing through three layers of biometric authentication, we entered a space that bore little resemblance to the historical castle above it.

"Welcome to my operations hub," I said, watching her reaction as she took in the array of cutting-edge technology.

Multiple monitors covered one wall, displaying everything from global news feeds to encrypted communication channels.

"This is impressive," Lex admitted, taking in the space with obvious appreciation. "Though I am curious as to why several of your systems are running outdated protection software."

"Deliberate vulnerability," I explained. "Honeypot to track intrusion attempts."

She appeared to understand and approve. "Smart. And the air-gapped systems?"

"For the most sensitive inquiries. Nothing connected to any network."

We settled into work, each leveraging our respective expertise. She navigated MI6's classified repositories while I activated my contacts across Europe and Asia. The functional rhythm we established surprised me—an unspoken understanding forming between two specialists with complementary skills.

At precisely twenty-two hundred hours, my secure communication system alerted me to an incoming connection. Lex raised her head when I accepted the call.

A heavily encrypted video feed appeared on the main screen, showing a person whose features were deliberately obscured.

"Infidel," the digitally altered voice greeted me. "I see you have company."

"She's cleared," I replied tersely. "What do you have for me, Kestrel?"

"Shipments of specialized neural processors through Hamburg, destined for a shell company in the Cayman Islands but diverted to St. Petersburg. Three such shipments in the past week."

"Quantities?"

"Enough to build a dozen prototype systems, based on what I understand of the technology."

"Any names associated with the receiving end?"

There was a pause, and I sensed Kestrel weighing how much information to sell. "This one's on the house, given our history. The paperwork referenced a research division headed by Dr. Viktor Orlov."

Beside me, Lex went rigid. "That's impossible," she said. "Orlov died in a laboratory explosion five years ago."

Kestrel laughed, the sound distorted by the voice modulator. "The rumors of his death were greatly exaggerated. He's very much alive and working on a project that has every spy agency from Moscow to Beijing scrambling to catch up."

"You're certain of this?" I pressed.

"I'd hardly say it if I weren't." While his image was pixelated, his head shake was visible. "Until next time," he said, abruptly ending the transmission.

Lex stood and paced the length of the room. "If Orlov is alive, we're facing a much bigger threat than we initially thought. He was brilliant but utterly without ethics. His neural-network designs were years ahead of their time, but he was censured for violating every standard of conduct in the field."

I checked the time—zero hundred hours. I'd been up for twenty-three straight, and given the exhaustion shadowing her eyes, Lex hadn't slept either.

"It's late," I said.

She rested against her chair and looked at her watch. "Yes, well, I suppose I should…"

Clearly, she hadn't made a plan for either staying in Scotland or returning to London, not that she'd be able to do that tonight.

"Stay at Blackmoor. I'll have a room prepared." As soon as I made the offer, I wondered how quickly I'd regret it.

She hesitated, then accepted. "Admittedly, I hadn't given it a thought. Your hospitality is appreciated."

I called Bastion and instructed him to prepare the countess's suite in a wing that was typically unoccupied apart from infrequent guests—although that hadn't applied to Fallon Wallace, who stayed in the part of the castle where my quarters were. A decision I now regretted.

"I'll show you there myself," I said once Bastion confirmed the suite was ready.

We walked in silence through the dimly lit corridors of Blackmoor, passing portraits of long-dead Carnegies. I wondered what my ancestors would make of me, the current earl, whose business dealings sometimes skirted the edges of legality.

"This is it," I said, opening the heavy oak door to reveal a spacious suite decorated in shades of blue and gold. Though traditional in style, it had been updated with modern amenities. "The bathroom is through there, and Bastion will have left everything you might need."

"Thank you." She looked around the room, her expression softening slightly. "It's beautiful."

"The countess's suite has always been considered the most elegant in the castle. Though there hasn't been a permanent occupant in years."

"No aspirations to change that?" she asked, a hint of teasing in her voice.

"None whatsoever," I replied more sharply than intended. "My work requires a singular focus."

She studied me with those perceptive eyes. "Or perhaps the recent betrayal has left its mark?"

"Good night, Dr. Sterling. I'll see you in the morning." I turned to leave, unwilling to discuss Fallon Wallace or my personal life.

"Con," she called, stopping me at the door. "Thank you for your honesty earlier. It makes working together…easier."

I acknowledged her words with a slight tilt of my head and left before I could say something foolish.

Rather than returning to my usual quarters, I made another impulsive decision and entered the earl's suite adjacent to hers. Traditionally, the earl and countess had connecting rooms, though the doors between them had remained locked, particularly before my parents' divorce.

The suite was maintained but seldom used—I preferred the modern comforts of my private wing, closer to the underground work area where I spent most of my waking hours.

As I lay in the massive four-poster bed, sleep remained elusive despite my fatigue as the woman in the room next door occupied my thoughts with unsettling persistence.

My mind, despite my best efforts to control it, conjured an image of her in that luxurious suite—her dark hair spread across the pillows like silk, her elegant frame draped in whatever she wore to sleep. Those perceptive eyes might be softer in the privacy of solitude, her professional armor temporarily set aside. I imagined the graceful curve of her neck, the delicate line of her collarbone, the smooth skin I'd glimpsed only at her wrists and face. The thought of her so close yet separated by centuries-old stone walls was a torment I hadn't anticipated.

This unexpected pull to the woman troubled me. My involvement with Fallon had ended with catastrophic professional consequences, reinforcing my lifelong belief that emotional entanglements were liabilities. Yet I couldn't deny my awareness of Lex's sharp intellect, her directness, and her unwavering confidence.

As I stared at the ceiling, it dawned on me that Lex herself wasn't the issue. The problem lay in my inexplicable failure to maintain the emotional distance I'd always established with women. Had Fallon's betrayal compromised something fundamental in my psychological architecture, creating vulnerabilities I hadn't recognized?

I needed to identify and neutralize this weakness. The Labyrinth threat demanded my complete focus— too many lives hung in the balance to permit distraction.

I turned onto my side, determined to find sleep, but instead of weapon schematics or Russian scientists, my mind filled with the memory of perceptive dark eyes that seemed to understand me without permission.

4

Lex

The ancient clock near the bedroom door chimed six times, pulling me from a surprisingly deep sleep. I lay still for a moment, orienting myself in the unfamiliar surroundings of Blackmoor Castle. The countess's suite. Conrad Carnegie's ancestral home. Project Labyrinth.

Despite my initial reservations about staying here—not that I'd had much of a choice—I'd slept better than I did in weeks. The suite was spectacular, elegant without being ostentatious, its decor complementing the original medieval stonework. For all his faults, Con Carnegie had great taste.

A knock at the door interrupted my assessment.

"Come in," I called, sitting up against the pillows.

A gentleman who appeared slightly older than Con and me entered carrying a silver tray. "Good morning, Dr. Sterling. I'm Bastion, Lord Blackmoor's butler. I've brought your breakfast."

"Thank you, Bastion." I watched as he set the tray on a small table by the window. Tea in a porcelain pot, fresh scones, clotted cream, and fresh berries.

"I've taken the liberty of ensuring the Wi-Fi details are beside your tablet," he said, indicating a small card on the tray. "Should you need to review any online information this morning."

While Con made sure I had access yesterday, I was impressed by the level of service despite the circumstances. I repeated my thanks.

"His lordship mentioned you might require a change of clothes." Bastion gestured toward a garment bag draped over a chair I hadn't noticed, along with a holdall on the floor next to it.

"That's very thoughtful," I said, genuinely surprised by Con's consideration. "Is Lord Blackmoor available this morning?"

"His lordship is in his offices with Mr. Drummond. Will there be anything else, Dr. Sterling?"

"No, thank you."

After he departed, I got out of bed to examine the clothing—simple but well-tailored trousers and blouses in neutral tones, along with a navy blazer that would complement my coloring. Practical choices, neither too formal nor too casual. Another unexpected insight into Con's character.

I ate while reviewing my notes on Project Labyrinth. The data we'd gathered so far pointed to a sophisticated AI-weapons system with potential global implications. The Tower-Meridian connection had opened the first door for us to understand the consortium's structure, but we still lacked crucial information about who made up the collective and their ultimate objectives.

What troubled me most was the speed with which Labyrinth was advancing. I was certain the shell companies Sullivan had traced to Tower-Meridian were now channeling funds toward quantum computing facilities and specialized neural processors. They had merely shifted operations without missing a beat after Fallon's death, suggesting her role, while significant, had been just one piece in a much larger structure.

The name being tossed about, at first in regard to her, was Janus. The mastermind. Only when we learned she was known instead as Chimera did we realize the horrific threat Labyrinth represented remained.

I finished my breakfast, showered, then prepared for the day, choosing the navy blazer, charcoal trousers, and a burgundy blouse from the options Con had provided. The fit was impressive—either a fortunate coincidence or evidence of a more detailed observation on his part than I'd realized.

Before leaving the suite, I ran a quick set of diagnostics on my mobile, checking for any signs of intrusion or monitoring. Working in Con's territory required caution, regardless of our temporary alliance. The scan showed no irregularities, but I activated an additional encryption layer as a precaution, then made my way through the castle's labyrinthine corridors toward the east wing. Portraits of Carnegie ancestors watched from gilt frames—stern-faced men and elegant women spanning centuries, their eyes seeming to follow my progress through their domain. The ancient structure felt like a physical manifestation of Con himself—imposing, complicated, with secrets hidden beneath its surface.

The modern defensive technology he'd introduced me to yesterday presented a stark contrast to the historical surroundings. Each checkpoint required increasingly complex verification methods that I hoped I'd remember how to activate.

After passing through the final barrier, I entered Con's underground operations hub to find him deep in conversation with a man I recognized as Angus Drummond. I'd met Gus briefly during the Tower-Meridian investigation, though we hadn't worked closely together. Where Con was all intensity and sharp edges, Gus projected a quiet competence that inspired immediate trust.

"Good morning," Gus said, standing as I entered.

"Dr. Sterling," Con acknowledged, his gaze lingering longer than strictly necessary. "I trust you slept well?"

"Better than expected," I admitted. "Though not everyone starts their day before zero five hundred hours."

His mouth curved slightly at one corner. "Time waits for no one, especially when chasing Russian scientists who should be dead."

"Any progress with that?" I moved to stand beside them, glancing at the financial data scrolling across one of the multiple monitors.

"Gus has been tracing potential funding sources," Con explained. "Following the money might lead us to the consortium's infrastructure."

"These transactions originate from the same accounts Sullivan linked to Tower-Meridian," Gus added, pulling up a digital chart. "But instead of funneling money through their humanitarian aid fronts, they've created new shells specifically focused on research facilities. The financial architecture is identical—they're using the same distribution methods Sullivan uncovered, just with different endpoint accounts."

I was impressed by his competency. The analytical framework Gus used was a painful reminder of Dr. McLaren's methodologies. My mentor would have appreciated his thoroughness. A momentary flash of doubt crossed my mind—what would Evelyn do with this data?—before I pushed it aside. I was on my own now, and I'd navigate this investigation my way. "You're looking for microtransactions that aggregate over time rather than large, suspicious transfers. Smart."

"Exactly." Gus's eyes flashed. "Tower-Meridian's fall—via Chimera's death—left numerous financial channels vulnerable. Someone's been exploiting them systematically."

I watched as the two men exchanged theories, finishing each other's sentences and communicating with minimal words.

"Incoming call," Con announced as an alert flashed across the main screen. "It's Ash."

The display shifted to reveal a striking blond man with piercing green eyes alongside a dark-haired woman I recognized as Sullivan Rivers, the investigative journalist whose work had helped expose Tower-Meridian. The scene behind them revealed they were in an ornate study, all dark wood and leather-bound books—the quintessential Scottish estate library.

"Morning." David Evans—code name Savior, though everyone seemed to call him Ash—greeted us. His voice was measured and direct. "Thanks for reaching out, Con."

"Appreciate you getting back to me so quickly," he replied, shifting slightly closer to the screen before turning to Gus and me. "I sent a message, asking if Ash and Sullivan could meet with us this morning. I thought a firsthand account would be more valuable than my summarizing."

"Dr. Sterling," Sullivan said with a slight wave. "Good to see you again."

The diamond on her left hand caught the light as she adjusted her position. "Likewise. I understand congratulations are in order regarding your engagement."

She smiled. "Thank you. I'm still getting used to the idea myself." The way she glanced at Ash spoke volumes about their connection.

Con cleared his throat, drawing my attention back. The subtle tension in his jaw suggested he was uncomfortable with personal topics. "I was hoping you could verbally brief Lex about the tunnels beneath Ashcroft Castle."

Ash leaned closer to the screen. "Of course. Though I wasn't aware of them until Con discovered them while updating the security infrastructure of Thistle Gate, the cottage closest to the shore of Loch Fyne." He paused briefly. "At the time, I didn't believe the tunnels were viable anymore." He glanced at Sullivan. "Sully, perhaps you should tell Dr. Sterling what you found."

She leaned closer to the camera. "Right. Based on records found in the former monastery's library, there are tunnel systems that connect all three estates—Glenshadow, Blackmoor, and Ashcroft. They likely date back to the Jacobite rebellion." Her fingers absently traced the edge of an antique desk blotter.

"I'm still not convinced they exist in the suggested entirety," Con added, his shoulder brushing against mine as he adjusted his position. The brief contact sent my pulse racing. "And if they do, like Ash mentioned, their viability is questionable."

"We discovered the Ashcroft ones were—" Gus began, but stopped when Con shifted in his chair and their eyes met. Interesting.

The dance of half-truths was familiar territory in our line of work, but something about this particular evasion bothered me. Omissions from people who were supposed to be allies in what could be the most significant threat to humankind we'd faced in years didn't sit well. We didn't have time for territorial games.

"What exactly are you trying to hide?" I asked directly, looking between the faces on the screen and then to Con beside me. My tone carried the edge of someone who'd navigated enough bureaucratic mazes to recognize deflection when I heard it.

Ash cleared his throat and seemed about to speak, his expression shifting to one of reluctant admission, when Con intervened.

"What we're not saying," Con admitted, running a hand through his dark hair in a rare display of discomfort, "is that Fallon was the one who found the monastery records at Glenshadow, then shared them with Sullivan." His voice tensed slightly at the mention of her name. "And the way we know the tunnels beneath Ashcroft are viable is because that's where Fallon took Sullivan after abducting her from the library in Ashcroft Castle. We haven't explored them enough to know the state they're in beyond that section."

I considered Con's words silently, mentally mapping the new information against what I already knew. The MI6 briefing on Tower-Meridian had mentioned Sullivan's abduction and Fallon's death, but it didn't contain additional details about the monastery records or the underground network's extent. The idea that three aristocratic estates were connected by hidden tunnels dating back centuries was both fascinating and alarming.

"How long ago were these discoveries made?" I asked.

"Approximately ten days ago," Ash replied, his gaze steady but guarded. I suspected there were still elements of the story being withheld.

As the call was drawing to a close, an elderly man wandered into frame behind Ash and Sullivan.

"Has anyone seen my book on Scottish architectural history?" he asked, seemingly unaware of the video call. His tweed jacket and knotted tie spoke of old-world elegance. "I left it somewhere yesterday, and now, I can't—" He stopped, noticing us on the screen. "Oh. Good morning, Angus. Conrad." His eyes, sharp despite his apparently scattered demeanor, assessed me with unexpected keenness.

Mairi Drummond, Gus's mother and the head house-keeper at Ashcroft according to the files I'd reviewed, hurried in after him. There was something protective in her posture as she approached. "Ambrose, as I told you, Ash and Sullivan asked not to be disturbed," she scolded with the familiar exasperation of someone who'd had this conversation many times before.

"It's all right, Mairi," David interjected with quiet reassurance.

I observed how the woman's demeanor subtly shifted as she addressed the older man. She was polite but spoke in the same way one might with a child or a difficult relative—patient but with an underlying tension. She shook her head and sighed. "The book you're looking for is in the front sitting room on the side table near the fireplace."

"Ah, thank you, Mairi." He wandered off again, seemingly lost in thought.

After exchanging a few more pleasantries and agreeing to share any new developments, the call ended, leaving the three of us in Con's operations hub surrounded by the soft hum of advanced technology.

"That was Ambrose Ashcroft," Gus explained, catching my questioning look. "David's slightly eccentric uncle. He occasionally lives on the estate." Something in his tone suggested there was more to it, but he offered nothing further.

The tunnel story continued to turn over in my mind. However, I couldn't allow myself to get distracted by historical curiosities. We needed to follow up on Con's source claiming Orlov was still alive, determine his connection to the neural processor shipments, and establish whether any of this related to Labyrinth. The thought that he'd possibly survived the explosion gave me a chill—his neural research had been revolutionary but deeply controversial.

"If there's nothing else we need to address now, I think I'll head back to Ashcroft," Gus announced.

Con stood, rubbing the back of his neck, where tension had clearly built during long hours of work. "We'll pick this up tomorrow. Zero seven hundred?"

Gus raised a brow. "Let's make it zero eight hundred since it's New Year's Day, ya old taskmaster." He waved to both of us before departing, the hub's doors sliding shut behind him with a soft hiss.

I was sure Con had forgotten it was a holiday, given I had too. However, in our line of work, there was no such thing as a day off in the midst of a mission.

Con turned to me, fatigue evident in the lines around his eyes despite his composed expression. In the artificial light of the operations hub, shadows accentuated the angles of his face. "Would you like to tour Blackmoor's grounds? We could both use some fresh air."

The invitation surprised me. I'd expected Carnegie to retreat to whatever private space he maintained in this ancestral fortress. I composed my features, not wanting to reveal my reaction. Perhaps a walk would clear my mind and help me understand my enigmatic colleague better. And maybe, just maybe, we could establish enough trust to work together effectively against the looming threat we faced.

That spending time with him unrelated to the mission held more appeal than I cared to admit was hard to acknowledge, even to myself.

5

Con

"Shall we?" I asked as we exited the ops hub. Fifteen hundred hours on the last day of the year, and instead of preparing for reconnaissance or running combat scenarios with my team, I was offering to show Lex the grounds of my ancestral home.

Her unexpected smile of agreement caught me off guard. Something about the woman continually surprised me, though I'd never admit it aloud.

"A walk would be welcome after being underground all morning," she said, pulling on the coat that was part of the wardrobe ensemble I'd had Bastion and Mrs. Thorne acquire for her, reminding me she'd probably want to return to London later today or tomorrow. Perhaps there was even someone there she'd want to celebrate the holiday with. It troubled me that the thought left me bereft. Perhaps I was getting lonely now that I was over thirty. I rolled my eyes. Good God, who was I?

"Everything okay?" she asked as we reached the main level of the fortress that had suited my ancestors far more than it ever did me.

"Fine, fine," I reassured her, resting my hand on the small of her back as we stepped outside, and I motioned to the stone path that wound around the eastern wall.

The winter sun hung low in the sky, casting long shadows across the landscape that looked barren at this time of year. The bite of Highland winter filled my lungs, a welcome change from the recycled air of my underground workspace.

"The original structure dates back to the thirteenth century," I explained. "The Carnegie name wasn't attached to it until the late fifteenth century, when my ancestor, Charles Carnegie, was granted the land and title by James III of Scotland."

Lex listened intently, her dark eyes scanning the stone battlements that rose against the sky. "And you've modernized it significantly, I assume? Beyond the technological additions."

"Each generation added their mark. My father installed proper heating in the east wing, thankfully. I've focused on the infrastructure—wiring, plumbing, connectivity—without disturbing the historical elements."

We rounded a corner toward the dormant western gardens, where a family of red deer grazed at the forest's edge, untroubled by our presence.

"The estate borders are remarkable," I continued. "Blackmoor shares boundaries with both Glenshadow and Ashcroft. The three properties form almost a triangle, with only a few miles separating each of the castles."

"And that's how you all became friends? The four of you—you, Ash, Tag, and Gus?"

I smiled, remembering the summers spent racing between the properties, exploring every inch of the combined territories. "Our families had connections going back generations. We were thrown together at various functions from the time we could walk. When we were around eight, our parents began allowing us more freedom to visit each other. We'd spend entire holidays together, rotating between the estates."

"Sounds idyllic, but how does Gus fit in?" she asked.

"That's complicated."

Her eyes scrunched. "Oh, my apologies."

"Not at all. However, if I tell you the story, you must swear not to repeat a word of it."

"I wouldn't want you to betray a confidence."

"It's just that it isn't common knowledge yet, although I suspect it soon will be."

Her smile was that of someone about to learn a great secret, which I suppose she was.

"As it turns out, after Ash's grandmum died, his grandfather had a great love affair with the housekeeper, Agnes. Some months later, along came Mairi…"

She gasped. "Which means Gus is Ash's cousin?"

"Correct."

"That's brilliant!" The smile left her face. "You said it isn't common knowledge."

"Mairi knew, of course, but Ash and Gus didn't until Christmas."

"This year?" she asked.

"That's right. It was actually Ambrose who let it slip. I suppose he thought Ash had figured it out at some point, which he obviously hadn't."

"Mairi is the housekeeper now?"

I confirmed it. "Not that Ash wants her to be. In fact, he tried to talk her into joining us for Christmas dinner. However, there's the matter of the rest of the staff. Ash wanted her to tell them in her own time."

"That's nice of him. Both parts."

"Yes, well, Ash is, above all things,…nice," I offered.

"When he isn't assassinating people."

I laughed out loud. "No, I suppose his victims wouldn't think so."

"I bet the four of you were hellions."

"Quite. We were determined to uncover every secret, climb every tree, and generally cause as much havoc as possible."

She laughed like I had. "Boys and their mischief."

"We were legendary," I admitted with a half smile. "What about you? Were you always the serious academic, or did you have your wild days?"

"I was insufferably straightlaced," she said with surprising candor. "The girl with her nose always in a book. Top of my class, perfect marks, never broke a rule." She kicked at a small rock on the path. "I didn't know how to be anything else."

Her admission stirred something unexpected in me—curiosity about the woman behind the professional façade. What would it take to loosen those tightly held restraints? What would Lex be like with her inhibitions lowered, free from the structure she seemed to cling to?

When I looked up, I found her watching me with an intensity that suggested she'd followed my thoughts. Heat flared between us, unexpected and unwelcome. She broke eye contact first, suddenly fascinated by a stone gargoyle perched on a nearby wall.

"Do you know much about the history of Scottish noble houses during the Jacobite era?" I asked, steering us toward safer ground.

"Only the basics. Many Highland clans supported the Stuarts, while others allied with the Crown. After Culloden, there were brutal reprisals."

I guided her toward a section of the castle that jutted out at an odd angle from the main structure. "This wing was added during that period. The eastern wing was damaged during a skirmish in 1745 when government forces suspected the Carnegies of harboring Jacobite fugitives."

"Were they?" Her eyes sparkled with genuine interest.

"Family legend says yes, but there's never been definitive proof. My grandfather used to tell stories about secret chambers and escape tunnels built throughout the castle." My eyes opened wide at the same time hers did. "I didn't think about it until just now."

She stopped walking. "Did he say how to access them?"

"Sadly, no, which was one reason I figured he was telling tales." My mind raced, trying to remember anything else my grandfather might have said that I'd passed off as fanciful. "Would you like to see some of the older sections of the castle?"

"I'd love to."

We circled back toward the main entrance, the temperature dropping as the sun dipped lower.

"Some of the original sections remain."

"How fascinating," she said, removing her gloves and tucking them into her coat pockets. "Thank you for these, by the way."

"I credit Mrs. Thorne entirely. There are times I swear she's a sorceress. As evidenced by her ability to pull together an entire wardrobe overnight."

Lex stopped walking for the second time. "But…"

I turned to look at her. "What?"

"Nothing. I just thought…never mind. It's not important. Many thanks to her and to you."

My mouth gaped when I connected the dots. "*Good God*, you didn't think they belonged to Fallon."

"*No!* I swear that never entered my mind. I just thought maybe. I don't know. You had women's clothing on hand."

I chuckled. "Just lying about? In your size?"

"When you put it that way, it was daft of me."

"No, Lex, everything was chosen just for you." We both froze when I—without thinking—wrapped my arm around her shoulders as I spoke. "Err, apologies," I stammered, quickly dropping it and stepping away.

"It's okay," she said just above a whisper.

I cleared my throat. "So, had enough, or shall we carry on?"

Her smile returned. "Carry on, please."

I guided her through the Great Hall, with its soaring ceilings and ancient tapestries, past the formal dining room where generations of Carnegies had entertained royalty and dignitaries, and down a narrow corridor that led to the oldest part of the castle.

"Mind your head," I warned as we descended a short flight of worn stone steps. The passageway narrowed, the ceiling dropping to a height that would have been comfortable six centuries ago, when people were considerably shorter.

"This section hasn't been renovated?" Lex asked, running her fingers along the rough stone wall.

"Minimal interventions for structural stability and lighting. Otherwise, it's as it was."

We entered a small chamber with an even lower, vaulted ceiling. Empty sconces lined the walls, though modern lighting had been discreetly installed to illuminate the space.

"What was this room used for?" she asked, moving toward the far wall.

"Storage, primarily. Though during clan uprisings and conflicts, it served as a shelter." I joined her where she stood, examining what had captured her attention. "What do you see?"

"The stonework is different here. See how the masonry shifts?" She traced the outline of what appeared to be a sealed archway. "This was an entrance to something once."

I studied the wall with fresh eyes. She was right. The stones were set differently, suggesting an opening that had been deliberately filled in. "Could be a doorway that was sealed during renovations."

"Or access to tunnels."

"Possibly. However, we won't be busting through the rock today," I teased, checking my watch. "We'd need proper tools and time. But it's certainly fascinating."

As we made our way back upstairs, I contemplated showing her the library next. I'd considered working there yesterday, before I granted her access to my ops hub.

"The library?" I suggested. "It's adjacent to where we first met, if you recall. Before I finally decided to trust you with my real work area."

Her lips curved into that knowing smirk I was beginning to recognize. "You mean after I bypassed your defenses and saw more than you intended?"

If there was ever someone who could break them—not the ones in my hub, but the ones I'd never let anyone get past, not even Fallon—it was the woman whose present gaze seemed to penetrate the deep recesses of my soul.

"A momentary oversight on my part," I replied, leading the way down the corridor. "Though I'm still not convinced you didn't have help."

"Would it wound your pride less if I had?"

"Perhaps."

The library doors stood open, welcoming us into a two-story chamber lined with books from floor to ceiling. A fire burned in the massive stone hearth, casting a warm glow across the leather bindings and gilded spines.

"This is magnificent," Lex said as she took in the shelves and shelves of books. "How many volumes?"

"Around twenty thousand, though I've never counted. Many are first editions. The collection has been in the family for generations."

She moved to the nearest shelf, running her fingers lightly across the spines. "Do you have historical documents as well? Records from the Jacobite period, perhaps?"

Her question sparked an idea. "We might. The family archives include journals, letters, and various documents dating back centuries." I crossed to a section farther from the fireplace, where older volumes were kept.

For the next hour, we lost ourselves in dusty tomes and fragile manuscripts, spreading our findings across the massive oak table that dominated the center of the room. The search became almost companionable, the earlier tension I'd caused by touching her with such familiarity fading away.

"Look at this," Lex said, gently turning the pages of a leather-bound journal dated 1744. "Your ancestor, Robert Carnegie, mentions 'secure passages that were used to transport loyal men and supplies without detection.'"

I leaned over her shoulder, reading the faded script. "And here, he references a map kept by the monks at Glenshadow."

"This is brilliant," she said.

Our faces were inches apart as we examined the text. "Quite."

She looked up suddenly, our proximity registering as her eyes met mine. Neither of us moved for a moment.

"This is proof the tunnels were used during the uprising," she finally said, her voice slightly lower than before. "They would have been vital during the uprising. Oh!" Her face scrunched.

"What?" I repeated, straightening and putting distance between us when her subtle perfume and the warmth radiating from her body made me want to touch her far more intimately than I had earlier.

"It should've dawned on me when you mentioned your ancestor was deeded the land by James III. I'm usually quicker on the uptake, so to speak."

While I didn't say it out loud, I'd known how my family acquired the land for most of my life, yet it had never occurred to me that it so obviously meant they were affiliated with the Jacobites.

"I have another question."

"Go on," I said.

"Fallon abducted Sullivan and took her into the tunnels, where she, Fallon, was ultimately killed."

I paced toward the window, watching darkness settle over the grounds. "Your question is, how did she know about them?"

Lex closed the journal. "Sullivan mentioned finding records at the monastery."

"We should visit tomorrow to see what else they might reveal."

The mention of Fallon had shifted the atmosphere, bringing reality crashing back into our historical treasure hunt. I found myself staring at the darkened landscape, my thoughts turning inward.

"She was skilled at finding vulnerabilities," I said quietly, more to myself than to Lex.

"Ms. Wallace?"

I gave an affirmative jerk of my head without turning. "In systems. In people."

Lex remained silent, but I sensed her watching me, evaluating whether to pursue the topic or let it drop. She chose the former.

"She must have been extraordinary to gain your trust," she said. "That doesn't strike me as something you give easily."

I laughed without humor. "I give it rarely and apparently with poor judgment."

"We all misjudge people sometimes."

"Not in my position. Not with the stakes involved." I turned to face her. "My failure to see through her could very well have resulted in the advancement of a weapons system with the ability to forever alter global stability."

Lex approached slowly, stopping a few feet away. "How long were you involved?"

"Days." The admission felt like pulling a splinter—sharp, then relieving. "Yet long enough that I should have recognized the inconsistencies. The information that never quite aligned."

"No doubt she was trained to compartmentalize," she said. "To maintain covers that withstand scrutiny. You can't blame yourself for her deception."

"Can't I?" I moved away from the window, needing to occupy my hands. I selected a bottle of Scotch from the sideboard and poured two glasses. When she accepted the one I offered, I raised mine. "To better judgment in the coming year."

"It is New Year's Eve, isn't it?" She glanced at her watch. "I'd lost track of the time. It's almost midnight."

"Not how either of us expected to spend it, I imagine. I don't suppose you…"

"What?"

"Had, have, someone…" Why couldn't I bring myself to actually ask?

"No." She lowered her gaze. "I'd much prefer working on a classified operation in a Highland castle with a temperamental earl, regardless." She smiled slightly.

I returned the grin despite myself. "And here we are."

"Right." She raised her glass. "To the new year. May it be less eventful than the last."

"Good riddance to this one," I declared, taking a drink.

Her expression softened slightly. "It wasn't a banner year for me, either."

I waited for her to elaborate, but she merely sipped her Scotch, her gaze drifting to the fire. The shadows played across her face, highlighting the curve of her lips. Despite my better judgment, I found myself wondering again what lay beneath her composed exterior.

The clock on the mantel chimed midnight, marking the arrival of the new year.

"Happy New Year," I said, raising my glass one final time.

"Happy New Year," she echoed, touching hers to mine with a soft clink. "I should probably head to my room. It's been a long day."

She finished her drink and set the glass down. "Thanks for the tour and the history lesson. It was…illuminating."

"I'll join you, err. I mean I'll retire as well. To my room."

We walked in silence through the castle corridors, the only sound our footsteps on stone and the occasional creak of ancient timber. When we reached the countess' suite, I paused.

"Good night, Lex."

"Good night, Con."

I turned toward the earl's rooms a few paces away, conscious of her gaze following me. At my door, I glanced back to find her still standing there, her expression unreadable in the dim light. For a moment, neither of us moved.

Was she thinking about the proximity of our beds, separated only by an ancient stone wall? The thought had certainly crossed my mind, unwelcome but persistent.

She broke the spell first, crossing the threshold without another word. I entered my own *temporary* suite moments later, closing the door on the strange tension that seemed determined to follow us despite every logical reason to resist it.

The new year had officially begun, bringing with it new challenges. Tonight, I needed distance and clarity that apparently even the sprawling castle couldn't provide.

6

Lex

The shrill ring of my mobile pierced the early morning silence, jolting me from a restless night. I fumbled for it on the bedside table, blinking at the time. Zero five fifteen.

"Viper." I recognized the secure line identifier before answering.

"Tell me I didn't wake you, the woman who never sleeps beyond zero four hundred." Bellamy Hall's voice held unmistakable amusement. "Not to mention, you're still in Scotland, I assume, and I haven't received an update on your investigation."

I sat up, suddenly alert. "Apologies, I—"

"Please, Lex. I'm joking. Tell me, how is Lord Blackmoor?"

"We've made significant progress—"

"On what precisely?"

I rested my head on the pillow. "Stop it."

"Forgive me for thinking you'd succumb to Infidel's charms."

I had, as she probably well knew or at least sensed, not that I'd admit it.

"Have you *also* made progress on the Project Labyrinth investigation?"

"What do you know about Viktor Orlov?" I asked instead of engaging in her suggestive comments.

"Rumor is he survived the explosion that was supposed to have cost him his life. However, I've not seen proof yet. What makes you ask?"

"I heard it as well." I moved to the window, watching dawn break over the Highland landscape. "I'd like to consult with Dr. McLaren," I blurted before I could talk myself out of it. Con certainly hadn't consulted with me about Angus Drummond's involvement or David Ashcroft's, Sullivan River's, or Niall MacTaggert's. Why should I feel compelled to check with him before working with people I had for years?

"You're right.," said Viper. "If Orlov is alive, Evelyn may very well have contacts who can confirm it one way or another."

"No doubt Dr. McLaren could provide insight on the list we're building of Fallon Wallace's contacts in Syria."

"You don't need my permission, Lex. This is your investigation, and McLaren is your contact as much as she is mine."

"Understood. It's just that…"

"Go on."

"Infidel was opposed to us adding anyone to the investigation who wasn't thoroughly vetted."

"Thoroughly vetted? Did you inform him—"

"I did, and while he backtracked slightly via an apology, he didn't go beyond that to say he was comfortable with my consulting with her."

"Tell him to sod off," Viper replied sharply. "You don't answer to him or to anyone from Unit 23 in the same way they don't answer to me. Request approved. Anything else pertinent?"

"The Blackmoor Estate is allegedly connected to Ashcroft and Glenshadow via underground tunnels."

"The same tunnels where Fallon Wallace was killed?" she asked.

"Yes, but they appear quite complex, based on the drawings I've seen thus far."

"Intriguing. Anyway, I had another reason to call."

"Go on."

"I've someone else I'm recommending join the team. No doubt Infidel will be opposed to him as well."

"Who?"

"Malcolm Bennett."

The man's reputation preceded him—thirty years in SIS, specialized in Russian operations, rigid adherence to hierarchical structures. Frankly, the recommendation puzzled me.

"I need to run. Do check in occasionally, Lex," she said before I could question what she thought Bennett would add.

"Yes, ma'am," I responded, not that she'd heard me before ending the call.

While not directly calling me out on it, Viper's questions about the investigation hit home anyway. I'd allowed myself to be drawn into Con's world, seduced not just by the man himself but by the mystery surrounding his ancestral home. My primary mission—which should be investigating Viktor Orlov's possible survival and his connection to the AI-weapons system—had taken a back seat.

Why did Carnegie affect me this way? I'd worked with brilliant men before without losing focus. I prided myself on my professional detachment, yet something about his intensity, his intellect, and his vulnerability regarding Fallon's betrayal…moved me. God, what was wrong with me?

In all the years I'd known her, Dr. McLaren never slept beyond zero five hundred. In fact, I'd developed the same habit while working with her. In the same way I'd forced myself to mention her to Viper without taking the time to talk myself out of it, I called her.

"Margot," she answered on the second ring. "How lovely to hear from you."

"I hope I'm not calling too early."

She chuckled. "You know better. However, I suppose once I get used to this retirement thing, I may allow myself to sleep in."

"Fat chance," I teased.

"Right you are, dear. Now, tell me why you're calling."

"I'm in the midst of an investigation and was wondering if I could talk you into a consult."

"Of course, and it's never something you have to talk me into. However, I'm on holiday in Scotland presently. Can it wait until I return to London?"

"Yes, it can wait, but it just so happens I'm in Scotland too."

"How lovely. Whereabouts?" she asked.

"Near Tarbert, at Blackmoor Castle."

She gasped. "You're joking. I'm over at Ashcroft."

"You are?" I gasped like she had. "What ever are you doing there?"

"I've known the family for decades, dear. I met Alexandria, who married the Duke of Ashcroft, at university, as well as the duke's brother, Ambrose. That's who I'm visiting."

I thought about Ambrose wandering into the library while Con, Gus, and I were video-conferencing with Ash and Sullivan. He hadn't mentioned having a guest, but why would he have done?

"Perhaps we could get together tomorrow?" I asked.

"Of course. Let me check with Brose to see if he has anything planned, and I'll get back to you."

After thanking her, I rang off, feeling far better than before our call. Con would just have to accept the fact that I'd made arrangements to meet with Dr. McLaren and didn't need his permission to do so.

I showered and dressed quickly, determined to regain my equilibrium. By zero six hundred, I'd made my way to the dining room, surprised to find it empty save for a breakfast spread and the always present tea.

"Mrs. Thorne anticipated you might rise early." Bastion appeared at my shoulder, startling me. "Lord Blackmoor asked to be notified when you came down. He's in his study."

"Thank you, but there's no need to disturb him. I can manage breakfast on my own."

Bastion gave a slight bow and withdrew, leaving me alone with my thoughts. I was halfway through my first cup of tea when Con appeared in the doorway, bringing with him that peculiar energy that seemed to alter the air in any room he entered.

"You're up early," he said, pouring himself coffee.

"Viper called," I responded flatly.

"Ah." He studied me over his cup. "Is she anxious for your return to London?"

"More that I make progress on the Labyrinth investigation." I met his gaze, searching for his reaction. Something flickered in his eyes before he steeled his expression.

I was about to tell him about my meeting with Dr. McLaren when his mobile buzzed.

Glancing at the screen, his eyebrows lifted. "Interesting timing. Tag's invited us to Glenshadow for an early brunch. Ten hundred hours." He set the phone on the table. "It would be the perfect opportunity to examine the monastery records we discussed last night."

"It would be," I muttered more than said. Here I was, falling right back under Con's spell.

"Would that I could read your mind," Con said with a half smile.

"I assure you that you do not."

He chuckled. "Shall I accept or decline?"

I thought it over. "It is a holiday, after all."

"My thoughts exactly." He smirked. "Though I admit I'm curious about the segue."

"As I said, Viper rang. Also—"

"We'll be back on the job full throttle, so to speak, tomorrow. For today, we have some time to kill. Shall we retreat to the operations hub and work ourselves silly or go for a morning walk?"

"A walk. Definitely." Since we wouldn't be back at work per se until tomorrow, I decided to wait to tell him about the meeting.

When we arrived at Glenshadow a couple of hours later, Tag met us at the entrance. The old monastery loomed behind him, its stone walls and arched windows unchanged since medieval times.

"Con." Tag clapped him on the shoulder, then extended his hand to me. "Dr. Sterling. Best wishes for the new year."

"Same to you, and please, it's Lex," I corrected.

"Lex, then." His smile didn't reach his eyes. "Everyone's already here. And when I say everyone, I mean we have a surprise guest. Two, in fact."

For a fraction of a second, I feared he was about to say Viper was here. It would be just like her.

"Who?" Con asked.

I held my breath and let it out when, instead of my boss, Tag said, "Ambrose."

"What in the bloody hell?" Con gasped at the same time I did, albeit for an entirely different reason.

"I know. Given the number of invitations we extend to him—simply out of courtesy, not with the expectation he'll accept—he chooses today to force me to add additional places at the table."

"You said two guests."

Tag looked at me. "Right. Yes, he has a friend visiting. I believe you know her. Dr. McLaren?"

"You knew?" My eyes met Con's, and I bristled at the recrimination I saw in them.

"I only recently learned she was in the area, but I certainly wasn't aware she'd be here."

"Would you excuse us?" he said to Tag before leading me into an alcove. "You recently learned she was here? When was this?"

"I neither care for your tone nor do I owe you an explanation."

"We previously discussed—"

"No, Con, you shared your opinion, and I disagreed. It was not a discussion."

"Do you intend to talk to her about Labyrinth?"

"Of course I do."

"Against my wishes?"

I shook my head. "As I said, I don't owe you an explanation."

"Wait. There's something else," he said, grabbing my hand when I turned to walk away.

"What?" I snapped.

"Tag is worried about something."

Admittedly, I'd found Tag to be quite tense every time I saw him. I'd begun to think his tight shoulders and the way his gaze continually swept our surroundings were merely habits of a man accustomed to constant threat assessment. "What about?" I asked, softening my tone before quickly realizing we were in the midst of investigating a threat on par with the development of a nuclear bomb. "Err, I mean specifically."

"We'll find out later," he whispered, putting his palm on the small of my back as we left the alcove and entered the conservatory where brunch was being served. David and Sullivan sat by tall windows overlooking the estate grounds, deep in conversation. Gus perused the serving dishes at a buffet table, while Mairi Drummond stood nearby, talking with one of Tag's staff members.

Despite being invited as a guest, Mairi maintained a certain reserve that spoke of decades spent navigating the complex social hierarchy at Ashcroft. The recent revelation of her true relationship to the family seemed to have done little to erase her old habits.

I glanced around the room but didn't notice Dr. McLaren or the man I'd seen in the background of yesterday's video call. Seconds later, they entered through a set of French doors that led in from an out-door seating area.

"Margot!" Dr. McLaren approached, and we joined hands. "How serendipitous that you're here this morning."

I fought to steel my expression despite the turbulent emotions—relief at seeing my mentor, confusion at finding her here of all places, and the lingering hurt over her abrupt retirement that had left me feeling so adrift. Particularly since it came just as the Labyrinth investigation began.

"Dr. McLaren," I managed, accepting the older woman's embrace. "It's a lovely coincidence to see you here."

"Life is full of surprises, isn't it?" Dr. McLaren said with the enigmatic smile that had always preceded her most important lessons.

We cheek-kissed, then she turned to an older gentleman dressed in a tailored tweed jacket who was examining an antique pocket watch with unusual intensity.

"Brose, this is the woman I was telling you about earlier, my protege. Margot Sterling, meet Ambrose Ashcroft."

"Lovely to meet you," he said, taking my hand and kissing the back of it. As our eyes locked, I couldn't help but think he looked less like the eccentric uncle in person than I'd expected and more like a distinguished academic.

"Ambrose," Con greeted him. "I didn't realize you'd be joining us," he lied.

The older man smiled thinly. "Niall always invites me. I simply choose to accept when it suits me."

Tag appeared at Con's shoulder. "Ambrose has been pestering me again about selling him a few pieces from the east gallery."

"Still on about those, is he?"

Later, when we were well out of Ambrose's earshot, Tag confided, "He asks every time he visits. Same routine—claims they're crucial for some exhibition he's curating. I've told him for years they're not for sale."

"Persistent old codger," Con replied, his voice low. "Never quite takes no for an answer, does he?"

Sullivan approached, offering a welcome distraction. "Good to see you again, Lex. How are you finding Scotland?"

"Cold but captivating," I replied, watching as Tag drew Con aside, their heads bent in serious discussion.

Throughout brunch and in between topics of conversation with Dr. McLaren, who I was seated beside, I observed the group dynamics with both personal and professional interest.

These people—apart from Ambrose, my mentor, and me—operated as a unit, bonded by lifelong connections and shared secrets. Gus and David maintained a continuous awareness of their surroundings despite the casual setting. Sullivan, though newer to their circle, had adapted to their hypervigilance. Tag moved with contained power, every gesture precise. Once we were all seated, Mairi appeared to relax, morphing into the woman who'd watched the four men grow up and loved them all equally.

Ambrose remained the anomaly even with Dr. McLaren's company. He spoke knowledgeably on various subjects but occasionally drifted mid sentence, his gaze turning vacant before he resumed with a slightly different cadence. When questioned directly, his responses came after small but noticeable delays, as if processing it through some internal filter.

I caught him watching me several times, his assessment uncomfortably penetrating. When our eyes met, he merely smiled and returned to his meal.

Shortly after brunch, he announced they'd be returning to Ashcroft.

"I will as well," said Mairi, standing when he and Dr. McLaren did. "If you'll excuse me, I have a great deal to do before tonight's festivities."

"Festivities?" Sullivan questioned.

"Just a small gathering of local artists and friends—on behalf of Evelyn's visit, of course," Ambrose said with a dismissive wave. "Nothing that would interest any of you."

"We'll speak tomorrow," Dr. McLaren said, squeezing my hand before thanking Tag and following Mairi and Ambrose out.

"How bloody awkward was that?" Tag said, leading us out of the conservatory.

I couldn't have said it better. In fact, I expected, any moment now, that Con would also announce we were leaving, after which we'd continue our discourse about my consultation with Dr. McLaren. Not that I had any intention of backing down about it.

"Here is the library," Tag announced as we entered a room that, unlike Blackmoor's masculine space, had been preserved with the monastery's original character—soaring ceilings, stained glass casting colorful reflections cross ancient stone, and endless shelves of historical texts.

"I've pulled a few volumes that mention the tunnel systems," he said, motioning to several journals that were spread across a massive oak table. "Some date back to the 1720s."

For the next two hours, we pored over fragile manuscripts and architectural drawings.

"The network is more extensive than I realized," Con said, examining a partially obscured map. "If these markings are accurate, the tunnels extend beyond our three estates to several points along the coastline."

"Strategic for smuggling during the uprisings," Tag said. "The Jacobites were nothing if not thorough in their planning."

Sullivan leaned closer, studying the faded markings. "I've read about similar networks beneath Edinburgh and Glasgow. The scale of these secret passages throughout Scotland is remarkable."

"My grandfather used to tell stories about smugglers using these tunnels well into the nineteenth century," Tag added. "Though I always assumed he was exaggerating."

Con chuckled. "I said something similar to Lex about my grandfather. I thought he was batty. It's interesting to me that my father never mentioned anything about them. He had to have known." He traced an imaginary line on the ancient paper without actually touching it. "I wonder how many are still navigable. I would expect most would have collapsed or flooded over time."

By late afternoon, David and Sullivan departed for Ashcroft, followed shortly by Gus.

"Something is going on with Nightingale. Typhon is tight-lipped on whatever it is," Tag said, walking Con and me to the main entrance.

"Any theories?" Con asked.

Tag shook his head. "I've been unable to make contact. I've a bad feeling in my gut, as they say."

"I'll see what I can find out," Con offered.

"Appreciated," Tag answered gruffly.

I thanked him for inviting us to brunch when he continued walking with us out to Con's vehicle.

"Talk tomorrow?" Con said to Tag before opening my door.

"We should do," he responded.

I was anxious on the drive back to Blackmoor. More than I should be. Then again, like Tag, I had a bad feeling in my gut. I let my mind drift as I gazed out at dusk settling over the Highland landscape, the winter sky deepening to indigo as Con navigated the winding roads as someone would who'd driven them all his life.

"Will you return to London tomorrow?" he asked, breaking the silence.

The question caught me off guard. "I'd like to meet with Dr. McLaren, but afterwards, I suppose I should."

He kept his eyes on the road. "If you'd like, I can arrange the helicopter for you. Perhaps, err, just to collect anything you might need?"

His assumption that I would immediately return made my traitorous heart skip. "That's considerate, but I should focus on tracking down Orlov. I've been distracted by the tunnels when my expertise would be better applied to verifying whether he's truly alive."

And the fact that Labyrinth appeared to be developing advanced AI integration, I added in my head.

Con pulled through Blackmoor's gates, his profile illuminated by the dashboard lights. "You're right, of course." His knuckles whitened on the steering wheel. "Though something tells me the tunnels are relevant to Labyrinth's operations. A trip to Edinburgh might prove useful."

We were still in the car, discussing the logistics for my return to London, when my mobile pinged with an encrypted message. The sender field showed only scrambled characters. Heart racing, I decoded the contents, then felt ice flood my veins.

Your investigation into Project Labyrinth threatens interests beyond your comprehension. Cease immediately or face the consequences. Not everyone at Blackmoor is what they appear.

"What is it?" Con asked.

I handed him the mobile. His face hardened as he read the message. "Someone has your secure number."

"Yes," I whispered. "Someone who knows exactly where I am."

His protective response was immediate. "You're not going anywhere tomorrow." His fingers brushed mine when he returned the mobile. "Not until we identify who sent this."

Our eyes met in the dim light, tension shimmering between us that had nothing to do with the threat.

"How would anyone get my secure number?" I asked, desperately trying to focus.

"The same way you hacked my systems," he replied, his voice low.

We sat in silence, the weight of the threat hanging between us. Con leaned closer, and for a breathless moment, I thought he might kiss me. His gaze dropped to my lips, then moved back to my eyes.

I found myself swaying toward him, rational thought evaporating in the heat of his proximity. At the last second, we both pulled away, the spell broken by mutual caution.

"We should go inside," he said roughly, putting distance between us.

I managed a weak smile, struggling to compose myself. "Yes. Of course."

Bastion met us at the entrance, his impeccable timing almost suspicious. "My lord, Mrs. Thorne asked me to inform you that she's prepared a special meal for you and Dr. Sterling to be served in the formal dining room in two hours."

Con raised an eyebrow. "The formal dining room?"

"She thought it appropriate for the occasion, sir."

"What occasion?" I asked.

Bastion merely smiled. "I believe she felt it warranted, given Dr. Sterling's presence and, err, the holiday."

Con's expression indicated this was unusual but not unwelcome. "Please thank her."

When he suggested we freshen up and change for dinner, I welcomed the time alone as much as I dreaded it. I was no stranger to threats, but this one felt too close with too much information. What was the sender implying with, "Not everyone at Blackmoor is what they appear"?

I showered, momentarily contemplating begging off dinner, but thought better of it. Bastion made it sound as though Mrs. Thorne had made a special effort, and whether it was on my behalf or not, I couldn't be ungracious and skip the meal. In the closet where I'd put the clothes that were also a courtesy of Mrs. Thorne, I found a velvet maxi dress that was elegant and casual at the same time. Below it were a pair of flats that matched the dress and looked as comfortable as slippers.

As I descended the grand staircase, Con stepped out of a nearby room and waited at the bottom for me.

"You look lovely," he said, taking my hand in a way that made me feel as though I'd fallen asleep and my dreams landed me in a historical romance novel. Those thoughts were reinforced when we stepped into the formal room I'd only peeked in previously, and saw the massive chamber, with its vaulted ceiling and medieval tapestries, had been transformed into an intimate setting.

Near the windows overlooking the moonlit gardens, a small table had been arranged with candles and fresh flowers. The rest of the cavernous space remained in shadow, creating the illusion of privacy.

Bastion pulled out my chair with an air of elegance, and moments later, an older woman with kind eyes appeared, carrying a silver serving tray.

"Dr. Sterling, this is Mrs. Thorne." Con introduced us as she set a plate in front of each of us. "She's the reason this old place remains standing."

She smiled, and her cheeks flushed. "Lord Blackmoor is such a charmer," she said, looking over at me.

"It's a pleasure to meet you," I said warmly. "Thank you for the lovely wardrobe you arranged and for this beautiful dinner."

"You're most welcome, Dr. Sterling. I hope everything fit properly."

"Perfectly, actually. It's remarkable, given you hadn't yet met me."

She took a step back, gave a slight bow at the waist, and motioned to our plates. "Lord Blackmoor's favorite salad with blue cheese, pears, and walnuts."

He reached up and took her hand. "While I appreciate the formality, given the occasion, you haven't called me Lord Blackmoor in years, Helena."

"Yes, Con," she replied with motherly affection before giving him an odd glance, then excused herself, promising to return with the next course.

"She seems flustered," I observed once she'd gone. "Did I say something wrong?"

Con cleared his throat. "Not at all. It's just that…" He paused, looking uncomfortable. "When arranging your wardrobe, I may have consulted your MI6 file for your, err, vital statistics."

"My file?" I set down my fork. "You mean my complete dossier?"

His expression confirmed my suspicion. "I simply wanted to ensure everything would fit properly."

A strange chill settled over me. How many women had stayed at Blackmoor, requiring his staff to arrange for a change of clothing? How many had sat at this same table, enjoying Mrs. Thorne's special meal? Had this been his approach with Fallon as well? The thought made me ill.

"Are you all right?" Con asked, noticing my changed demeanor.

I set down my napkin. "Actually, I'm suddenly not feeling well. If you'll excuse me, I think I should retire."

"Lex—"

"Thank you for dinner." I rose quickly, avoiding his gaze. "Please give Mrs. Thorne my apologies."

I fled the dining room, mortification and an inexplicable sense of betrayal fueling my retreat. How could I have been so foolish? Con Carnegie was known for his strategic manipulation of situations and people. I'd allowed myself to become just another woman susceptible to his wily ways.

I was almost to my room when I heard rapid footsteps behind me.

"Lex, wait." Con's voice halted me in the corridor. "What happened back there?"

I turned, struggling to maintain my composure. "Nothing. I'm simply tired."

"That's not it." He stepped closer, eyes searching mine. "Something changed. Tell me what's wrong."

"It doesn't matter."

"It matters to me." His voice softened as he reached up, gently cupping my cheek. "I wish you'd talk to me."

The warmth of his palm against my skin melted my resistance. His touch was tentative, almost reverent— nothing like the calculated gesture I'd imagined.

"I wish I could," I whispered, my defenses crumbling beneath his gaze.

7

Con

I broke the fragile moment by stepping back, suddenly aware of our proximity in the dimly lit corridor. "Lex, about dinner...I apologize if I upset you."

She crossed her arms, her expression guarded. "It was nothing."

"It wasn't nothing. You left rather abruptly." I ran a hand through my hair, frustrated at how poorly this conversation was going. "Look, I only accessed your file for practical reasons. I wanted to ensure you had proper clothing that fit well. Nothing more."

Something shifted in her eyes, a flicker of understanding perhaps. "You could have asked."

"I could have, yes. I should have." I took a breath. "The truth is I find myself..." The words caught in my throat. This was territory I vowed I'd never explore again. "I find myself drawn to you in ways I hadn't anticipated. And after Fallon, I'm not—" I stopped, unable to finish the thought.

Her features softened. "We both have our reservations."

"Indeed." I let the silence stretch between us, unwilling to break it with platitudes or demands. "For what it's worth, I'm sorry."

She seemed to accept my explanation, her hand reaching for her door. "Good night, Con."

"Good night, Lex."

She disappeared into her room without another word, leaving me standing in the corridor, with my thoughts. I entered the earl's suite and closed the door behind me, leaning against it with a sigh, wondering why I was staying in what was essentially a guest room rather than in my own bed. "Because you want to be near her, you daft idiot," I admitted to myself.

Sleep eluded me again. I tossed restlessly, replaying our interaction. Did accessing her file truly bother her that much? Perhaps it was the implied invasion of privacy, though in our line of work, privacy was often an illusion. Then again, her MI6 dossier would contain personal details far beyond what was necessary to order clothing.

Had my admission of attraction further raised her ire? Bloody hell, what had I been thinking? Our focus needed to remain on Labyrinth. The stakes were too high for personal entanglements.

By zero six hundred, I gave up on sleep entirely and headed to my private gym. Physical exertion had always been my remedy for mental restlessness. After a punishing workout, I showered and dressed, determined to reclaim our professional rapport.

When I returned to the main level, I found Lex already in the dining room, studying her tablet while sipping tea.

"Good morning," I said, pouring myself coffee. "Sleep well?"

She looked up, her expression giving nothing away. "Well enough. You?"

"The usual." I took the seat across from her. "With the hope you may have changed your mind about leaving, I thought we might establish a more permanent workspace for you here at Blackmoor. The operations hub has a secondary station that's rarely used."

She looked up with interest and set down her cup. "It's kind of you to offer, and it would be helpful. I'd like to begin tracking down the rumors about Orlov."

"Of course." I spread marmalade on toast, keeping my tone deliberately casual. "Once we've finished breakfast, we'll get you settled."

We ate in silence before heading to the operations hub, where multiple monitors hummed as if to say they held answers to yet-unasked questions. Yesterday was an anomaly. Typically, if I was at Blackmoor, I came down here at least once a day. More accurately, I spent hours on end in what I considered my domain and no one else's. Yet here I was, setting Lex up in her own space. Why? Because if she could access everything she needed here, she wouldn't have to return to London to work. In other words, she wouldn't have to leave.

"This will be your work area," I said, gesturing to a sleek setup near mine. "MI6 and Unit 23 databases are available through secure channels."

She settled into the chair, immediately typing in access codes. "Impressive. Better than my setup at Vauxhall Cross."

I smiled despite myself. "Don't let Viper get wind of that."

For the next hour, we synchronized our systems to facilitate information sharing while maintaining the necessary firewalls.

"You've upgraded your firewalls since I arrived," she noted, eyes on her screen. "New encryption algorithm?"

"Developed it myself after your late-night demonstration." I couldn't help the smirk that crossed my face. "Care to test it?"

Her lips curved upward. "Perhaps later."

I pulled up a secure window and began typing. "While we have a moment, I wanted to show you what I've found regarding the message you received yesterday."

Her expression sobered immediately. "Any luck tracing it?"

"That's the problem." I displayed a complex network diagram on the main screen. "I've hit a wall. The message appears to have originated from within Blackmoor itself."

"How odd," she said, leaning closer.

"That was my initial reaction. I've spent hours trying to break it down. Routing suggests it was sent from our network, but I can't pinpoint a specific device or user."

"I tried tracing it from my end as well." She shook her head. "Nothing."

"It's some kind of elaborate looping coding designed to create a digital echo chamber that makes the source appear local." I closed the diagram with a frustrated gesture. "Whoever sent it has considerable technical skills."

"And access to my secure number," she added quietly. "Not to mention knowledge of my presence here."

Our eyes met, both acknowledging the disturbing implication.

"I'll keep working on it," I promised. "In the meantime—"

An alert appeared, indicating an arrival at the main gate. "Gus is here," I said, checking the feed. "Earlier than expected."

Minutes later, he joined us, carrying a leather portfolio. Despite his unassuming appearance, Gus was one of the sharpest financial analysts I'd ever met, with an uncanny ability to trace money through even the most convoluted channels.

"Morning," he said, greeting us both. "I've got something interesting. Oh, but first, Dr. McLaren asked me to tell you that she and Brose are spending the day in Stirling, followed by a visit to the Kelpies. She said she hoped you wouldn't mind."

"Of course not. Thanks for relaying the message." Lex appeared perplexed.

"Everything okay?" I asked.

"Just anxious, I suppose." She turned to Gus. "So, you said you had something interesting. Is it connected to Orlov?" Lex asked.

"Possibly." He spread several documents across the table. "I've identified a series of transactions between shell companies based in Cyprus, the Cayman Islands, and St. Petersburg. The amounts are structured to avoid triggering automatic monitoring systems."

I examined the data. "These originate from the accounts linked to Tower-Meridian."

"Yes, but I found something else." Gus pulled up a digital chart on the main display. "These transactions coincide exactly with Tower-Meridian's shipment dates Sullivan previously documented."

Lex moved closer, studying the data. "And the receiving accounts?"

"Registered to various scientific research entities, all with ties to a holding company called Nova

Perspectives. It's supposedly a private think tank specializing in AI applications."

"Never heard of them," I said.

"Unlikely you would have, given how deep their cover is. Also, while they were incorporated just eleven months ago"—Gus highlighted several transactions—"they've moved nearly forty million pounds through these channels in that time."

"These accounts here follow the exact dispersal pattern I saw in a classified op three years ago. Russia uses a similar structure," said Lex, pointing to a cluster on the screen.

"Yet some of these transactions originate from London," I noted. "Specifically, from IP addresses registered to…"

Gus finished my thought. "Firms in the financial district. Several prestigious ones."

A sudden alert flashed on my monitor, interrupting our discussion. I moved quickly to another terminal.

"Someone's probing the system," I muttered, activating countermeasures. "Sophisticated attempt, specifically targeting secured files related to Orlov."

Lex joined me, her shoulder brushing mine as she leaned in to observe. "Can you trace it?"

"Working on it." I initiated tracking while simultaneously strengthening our defenses. "They're bouncing through multiple proxies."

After several tense minutes, I had a location. "Edinburgh. Northern section of Old Town, near the university."

"That's a promising lead," said Gus. "Too much of a coincidence to dismiss."

I was already planning our next move. "Lex and I should investigate tomorrow. If Orlov is alive, he might have connections to academic circles where his expertise would be valued."

"I'll continue following the money trail," Gus offered. "See if I can establish actual connections between these shell companies and any properties or facilities in Edinburgh."

After Gus departed, Lex and I remained in the operations hub, crafting our approach for the following day.

"We should review the full dossier on Orlov," she suggested. "I knew him professionally before his supposed death."

I raised an eyebrow. "You never mentioned that."

"We crossed paths at several international AI conferences."

"And yet you defended him to Typhon."

She met my gaze steadily. "I did not. We were discussing Dr. McLaren."

"Right. My apologies." The look she gave me was as odd as I was feeling. Maybe the lack of sleep was finally catching up with me.

As evening approached, we ordered dinner to be brought to the ops hub rather than risk another awkward formal meal. Mrs. Thorne sent down a hearty stew with freshly baked bread that we ate while continuing our work.

"What drew you to this field?" I asked during a brief respite. "AI development, I mean."

Lex considered the question, her spoon hovering over her bowl. "The potential. Not just for weapons systems—though that's where my expertise lies—but for solving problems beyond human capability."

"And the ethical considerations?"

"Always present. That's what separates me from people like Orlov." She broke off a piece of bread. "What about you? How does an aristocrat end up as a cybersecurity expert and secret intelligence operative?"

"Sullivan's analysis of Tower-Meridian's shipping manifests wasn't just about missing supplies or diverted cargo," I explained. "Looking back at her data through the lens of what we know now, those discrepancies align perfectly with components needed for advanced neural processing. The 'medical equipment' she tracked wasn't being sold on the black market—it was being repurposed for Labyrinth's processing architecture."

"That explains your interest in this mission. But what I really want to know is how you got into this in the first place."

I smiled, surprised by my willingness to share after my diversion tactic had failed. "I was always fascinated by technology, even as a child. My father thought it a passing phase and expected me to focus on managing the estate. But when I hacked into my school's grading system at fourteen, he realized it might be more than a hobby."

"Did you change your grades?" Her eyes held a hint of amusement.

"God, no. I was top of my class already. I just wanted to see if I could do it." I laughed at the memory. "Though I did adjust the cafeteria menu to remove Brussels sprouts permanently."

"A noble cause." Her laughter joined mine, the sound warming me.

"After university, I was approached by government recruiters who'd been monitoring my…extracurricular activities. The rest, as they say, is classified."

The conversation continued flowing naturally. We discussed our respective work experience, our educational backgrounds, even our favorite books—finding unexpected common ground in our shared love of classical literature.

"Paradise Lost?" she asked, surprised. "I wouldn't have pegged you for a Milton enthusiast."

"The devil has all the best lines," I replied with a half smile. "You forget I first studied at Cambridge."

As midnight approached, I noticed her stifling a yawn.

"We should get some rest. Early start tomorrow if we're heading to Edinburgh." I stood and held out my hand, but she didn't take it.

She stretched in her chair. "I suppose you're right."

I found myself smiling as we made our way through the castle corridors. The evening had been unexpectedly pleasant—not just productive but personally satisfying in a way I hadn't experienced in some time. The time spent with Fallon was more about what I'd considered to be playful banter. In hindsight, "combative" would have been a better word for it.

At her door, she paused. "Thank you for today. The workspace, the collaboration…" Her voice trailed off.

"My pleasure." I stood closer than necessary. The magnetic pull between us was impossible to resist. "Sleep well, Lex."

She looked up at me, her dark eyes reflecting the dim corridor lighting. "You too, Con."

Neither of us moved for a long moment. The tension between us heightened, transforming into something more complex than simple attraction or professional respect. Was I naive to think this could be understanding and recognition—the rare connection between two people who saw each other clearly?

"We have an early start," I said, taking a deliberate step backward.

"Yes," she agreed, her voice equally quiet. "Good night, then."

I watched her disappear into her room before continuing to the one that wasn't my own but I couldn't bring myself to leave.

My thoughts were in disarray. The mission remained paramount—Labyrinth posed too great a threat to allow myself a distraction. Yet, as I prepared for bed, I couldn't dismiss the growing certainty that Dr. Margot Sterling had become far more than a professional ally in my mind.

God, how I wanted to unlock the adjoining door that separated us, climb in bed next to her, leave the mission behind, and get to know each other in the way I was certain fate intended.

8

Lex

Despite the late hour, once inside the room, I reached for my mobile. Viper answered on the third ring.

"Lex, is everything all right?" Her voice was crisp and alert.

"Yes. I, err, wanted to update you on our plans to visit Edinburgh tomorrow."

A brief pause hung between us. "That doesn't warrant a call at this hour."

"There's more." I lowered my voice. "Someone sent me a message. A threat."

That caught her attention. "Go on."

I recounted the words verbatim, explaining how Con had traced it to his own network.

"Curious," she said. "The part about 'not everyone at Blackmoor is what they appear' is quite ominous, isn't it?"

"My thought too. It could be trying to point me toward someone in Con's inner circle." I hesitated. "Or…"

"Or warning you about Carnegie himself," Viper finished. "I'll have MI6's technical division look into it. Keep your guard up, Lex."

"I always do. Oh, and you'll never guess who turned up."

"I've no idea."

"Dr. McLaren. Turns out she was friends with Alexandria Ashcroft as well as Ambrose. They attended university together."

"How interesting," she said in a way that told me she was likely tapping her lower lip with her index finger. "So, are you meeting?"

"We are, but I don't know when yet. She and Ambrose went to Stirling today."

"Yes, well, like I said, interesting. Keep me posted, Lex."

After ending the call, I stared at the ceiling. Sleep came reluctantly, and when it did, I dreamed of stone walls with secrets and dark tunnels that led nowhere.

Con didn't look up when I entered the dining room at zero six hundred and found him there, already sipping coffee. His attention was fixed on a tablet, giving me a moment to observe him unnoticed. The morning light streaming through the windows highlighted the strong line of his profile—the straight nose, the sharp cut of his jaw now shadowed with stubble, and those impossibly deep sapphire eyes focused intently on whatever he was reviewing. It was as though some Renaissance artist had decided to carve the perfect balance of strength and refinement, and the result was Conrad Carnegie.

His white dress shirt stretched across broad shoulders as he leaned forward, revealing the physical strength that matched his formidable intellect. I'd worked with attractive men before, but something about Con's particular combination of aristocratic elegance and raw power was uniquely distracting.

He raised his head but didn't speak. What was that all about? Here I was, ogling the man while he was giving *me* the cold shoulder.

Rather than ask outright what was wrong, I observed him as I poured tea.

"We should get on the road soon if you still intend to travel to Edinburgh with me," he said abruptly.

"Why wouldn't I?"

He set his cup down. "I thought perhaps you'd prefer to return to London."

"I'm baffled, Con. You're again assuming I want to return to London? Why would I have agreed to you setting up the workspace yesterday if that was my intent?" I studied his profile. "Unless you've changed your mind about our collaboration?"

"Not at all." There was something closed off in his manner that hadn't been there the night before.

"When will the helicopter arrive?" I asked, looking out the window to the pad where it usually sat.

"I prefer to drive. Traveling by air is too visible for what I have in mind."

The prospect of spending hours confined in a car with this cooler, more distant version of Con wasn't appealing, but I agreed anyway. "I'll be ready in fifteen minutes."

The drive began in strained silence. Beyond the windscreen, the Highland landscape rolled by, hills giving way to farmland as we moved southeast. After nearly an hour of neither of us saying a word, I couldn't bear it any longer. "Is there something you want to tell me, Con?"

He kept his eyes on the road. "Such as?"

"You've been…different since this morning. Are you still upset about me conferring with Dr. McLaren?"

"That isn't it."

I raised a brow. So there was something. "Go on."

His hands gripped the steering wheel more tightly than seemed necessary. "I received an alert last night. Someone from MI6 attempted to access my system." His eyes flicked to me briefly. "Unlike your successful breach, they failed."

The subtle accusation hung between us. "I assure you it wasn't at my request."

"I never suggested it was." He returned his gaze to the road. "Though the timing is curious, don't you think?"

"I suppose," I said under my breath.

For the remainder of the journey, we slipped into professional mode, discussing potential locations connected to the suspicious transactions Gus had identified. Con knew Edinburgh intimately, mapping out observation points and possible approaches to each target.

By early afternoon, we were staking out a high-end art gallery in Edinburgh's New Town. The elegant

Georgian building housed exclusive collections that, according to Con's research, frequently changed hands through private sales rather than public auctions. What made it even more interesting were the many well-dressed figures who came and went while we sat at a café across the street, watching the entrance.

"I haven't seen anyone I recognize from previous or current briefings."

"I haven't, either. However, it's the perfect setup for money laundering," he said as I sipped my tea. "Artwork values are subjective enough to justify almost any price."

After an hour with no significant activity, Con suggested we move to our next target—a private club with known connections to Russian business interests. Located in the Old Town, the club occupied a building with medieval foundations, its entrance discreet and unmarked.

"How do you propose we get in?" I asked as we observed from across the narrow street. "I doubt they welcome walk-ins."

The smile that curved his lips held a hint of mischief. "We won't be using the front door."

Con led me through a series of winding closes and *wynds*—narrow passages between buildings that dated back centuries. We descended worn stone steps into what appeared to be a dead end until he pressed against a particular section of wall.

"Edinburgh's underground history is one of its best-kept secrets," he explained as a hidden door swung inward. "The Old Town is built on layers of earlier structures. From what I read, if you know the paths, you can move beneath much of the city. That's not even taking the tunnels into account."

We navigated the damp passageway illuminated by the flashlight function on Con's mobile. The stone-work looked ancient, and water was seeping through in places, forming small rivulets along the floor.

After fifteen minutes, Con stopped, placing a finger to his lips. Above us, muffled voices became audible through what appeared to be a ventilation grate.

"The club's private meeting room," he whispered. "It's directly overhead."

We listened intently. The conversation was in English, but with heavy Russian accents. They were discussing shipments, delivery dates, and defensive protocols using coded language that, nonetheless, made their meaning clear to trained ears.

"The package from St. Petersburg cleared customs yesterday," one voice said. "We are pleased with the components."

"And the integration?" another asked.

"Progressing according to schedule. Our contact says we'll be ready for the demonstration within the month."

A new voice joined the conversation, Scottish and refined. "The consortium is growing impatient. We've invested considerable resources."

"Your impatience is noted but irrelevant," the first Russian voice replied coldly. "Our developer works at his own pace. Push him, and you risk everything."

Suddenly, a mobile rang above us, followed by a hushed conversation.

"Patrol identified intruders," the Scottish voice said.

Con gripped my arm. "We need to move. Now."

We retreated down the passage, but the footsteps overhead tracked our movement. A door somewhere ahead of us opened, light spilled into the tunnel, and Con pulled me into a small alcove barely large enough for one person to squeeze into, pressing me against the wall and covering my body with his.

In the darkness, every sensation was intensified—Con's heartbeat against my chest, the warmth of his breath on my neck, the tremor in his hands as they braced against the wall on either side of me. My own pulse raced, partly from danger but more from his proximity.

While one person stopped briefly, shining his light in our general direction, the alcove's depth kept us hidden in the shadows.

When the sound of footsteps faded, neither of us moved immediately. Con's eyes found mine in the dim light, questioning.

"We should go," I whispered, yet made no attempt to move.

"Yes," he agreed, his voice rough. Still, he remained where he was, his gaze dropping to my lips for a fleeting instant before he stepped back, releasing me from the confines of our hiding place and the spell of the moment.

We made our way back to street level in silence, both of us processing what we'd overheard—and what had nearly happened between us.

"We got what we came for," Con said, checking to see if the alleyway was empty before we emerged, blinking in the late-afternoon sunlight. "Time to return to Blackmoor."

"If the developer they mentioned is Orlov and he's preparing to test Labyrinth's capabilities, we're running out of time," I said once we were in the SUV.

Con nodded grimly.

"With Janus at the helm," I added quietly, the name sending a chill straight through me.

Just as Edinburgh faded from view behind us, Con's secure mobile buzzed with a distinct tone.

"Something from Kestrel," he said, passing it to me.

The message was brief but significant. *Confirmed Viktor Orlov alive. Brother Oruzhiye deceased.* "Good God," I muttered, then read it aloud.

Con gasped. "Viktor is *Oruzhiye's* brother?"

"According to Kestrel, yes." Sergei Orlov, whose code name meant "the Gun," had worked for the KGB for many years before becoming a freelance assassin. He was killed a few years ago in a shootout in Islamabad.

"Familiar with him?" Con asked.

"Isn't everyone?" I said under my breath, already scanning the files I could access via my secure mobile to see if I'd somehow missed the connection. "I first saw his name in a briefing that crossed my desk during an op I was supporting in Ukraine. He was ruthless, effective, and for sale to the highest bidder." I frowned. "Something he and his brother apparently have in common."

"If Viktor moved in his brother's circles, the consortium could be building a dangerous network," Con finished grimly.

We drove the rest of the way in silence. The clues we collected today were troubling yet got us no closer to Labyrinth.

When we arrived at Blackmoor, I was too exhausted to put two thoughts together.

"You should get some rest," Con said as we entered the castle. "It's been a long day."

"What about you?"

"I have some work to follow up on."

"Anything I can assist with?"

He shook his head. "Not necessary. We'll regroup in the morning."

The dismissal stung more than it should have. After our moment of connection in the tunnel, I'd thought perhaps the barriers between us were lowering. That no longer appeared to be the case.

As I climbed the stairs alone, disappointment mingled with doubt. The warning echoed in my mind—*not everyone at Blackmoor is what they appear.*

Not for the first time since arriving, I wondered how wise it was to trust Con Carnegie.

9

Con

I stared at my monitor, rage and frustration building as another trace program hit a dead end. For hours, I'd been trying to identify who from MI6 had attempted to breach my system, as well as the source of the threatening message sent to Lex. Everything I attempted had either led nowhere, the digital trails had looped back on themselves, or they had vanished entirely.

"Bloody hell." I pushed away from my desk and rubbed my burning eyes. I'd worked through the night, fueled by coffee and the determination that, now, left me drained and no closer to answers.

My mobile buzzed with a message alert in response to a text I'd sent to Gus, not expecting to hear from him until a more reasonable hour. To my surprise, he'd replied immediately.

Tag and I on our way. ETA 30 min.

I texted back a confirmation and headed upstairs to shower and change. The cold water revived me somewhat, though my thoughts remained sluggish from too many nights with either too little sleep or none whatsoever. By the time I returned to the ops hub, the two men were already on their way in.

"You look like hell," said Tag.

"Good morning to you too, arsehole." I gestured to the coffee station in the corner. "Help yourselves."

"Did you sleep at all?" Gus asked, handing me a fresh cup.

"Someone attempted a breach. I've traced it to MI6, but that's where it starts to loop," I said rather than answer his question. As much trouble as I was having putting a coherent thought together, I wasn't about to try to explain the real reason sleep had eluded me.

Tag's eyebrows shot up. "Related to Lex?"

"Uncertain." I took a long sip of coffee. "What's happening with Nightingale?"

Tag's face darkened as he sat in the chair opposite mine. "Still nothing. She's gone completely dark, and Typhon won't tell me a bloody thing."

The tension in his voice caught my attention. Tag was typically unflappable, yet Leila Nassar had clearly gotten under his skin.

Before I could comment, Lex walked in.

"Am I interrupting?" she asked.

"Not at all," I answered. "In fact, we could use your input."

"What's going on?" Lex sat in the chair near the workspace I'd set up for her. Just that very small thing made me happier than I'd felt in twenty-four hours.

"I'm concerned about Nightingale," Tag began, reiterating what he'd just said about his inability to make contact.

"It seems likely that something that happened or that she found in Syria has made her a target," Gus offered, leaning against a nearby console. "The question is, why did she leave that out of her briefing?"

"Fear?" Lex suggested. "Or perhaps she doesn't trust the channels available to her."

"Or she withheld information deliberately," I added.

"Someone could have gotten to her," Gus suggested.

Tag shook his head. "We've worked together for years. She knows she can trust me."

"Maybe that's the problem," Lex said quietly.

My eyes met hers, but she quickly looked away.

"I think there's something else going on," she added. "How close are the two of you?"

Tag shrugged. "We're friends."

Lex raised a brow.

"With occasional benefits," he said under his breath.

My mouth gaped. We'd been best friends all our lives, and he hadn't admitted as much to me.

"Maybe she's protecting you," Lex suggested. Once again, her eyes met mine only briefly.

Tag checked his watch and stood. "I need to see her. Talk to her in person. Typhon can damn well tell me where she is, or…"

"Or what?" I asked.

"I'm finished."

My eyes met Gus'.

"I'll come with you," he said, following Tag when he stood.

"Keep me posted," I said as they prepared to leave.

Lex stood too. "Tag? If Nightingale doesn't want to see you, respect her wishes."

I saw his struggle, recognized it from my own.

"Roger that," he finally said before the two men walked out.

Lex sat back down and turned toward her computer, but she didn't touch the keyboard. I pulled my chair closer to hers, leaned forward, and rested my elbows on my knees.

"I'm sorry."

She glanced over at me. "Is that a blanket apology, or is it for something specific?"

"Both?" I said, winking.

"What was it Mrs. Thorne said? 'Lord Blackmoor is such a charmer'?"

"Lex, I—"

"Don't. Let me speak first."

"Go ahead."

"I understand why you're hesitant to bring other people into the Labyrinth investigation, particularly given what happened with Fallon Wallace."

As hard as I tried not to, I still cringed.

"But what if I said I didn't want you to confer with Tag or Gus or Ash?"

"It would be impossible for me not to."

"Dr. McLaren was never my best friend, but I did—do—admire her in the same way I'm sure you do your friends. To suggest I not confer with a woman who taught me everything I know seems really unfair, Con."

I raised my head to look into her eyes. "You're right."

"Simple as that?"

"Yes."

"In that case, I know how you can make it up to me," she said with a smirk that made me want to pull her into my arms and kiss her pouty lips.

"How?" I asked, lowering my voice. "Whatever you want. I'll give it to you." The words came out exactly as I'd meant them, too suggestive perhaps, but I couldn't help it. I wanted this woman. Here and now.

"Take me out to lunch."

The effect her request had on my body was like a metaphoric record scratching. "Err, sure. Uh, did you have anywhere in particular in mind?"

"Do you have a favorite place?"

Right now, the only thing I could picture was her, in my bed, naked while I fed her.

"Con?"

"Uh, right. My favorite spot. There's the Stag's Head. It's a decent pub in the village."

"Perfect. I'll get my coat."

Twenty minutes later, we were seated in a corner booth of the sixteenth-century establishment that had served the village for generations. Oak beams crossed low ceilings, and a fire crackled in the stone hearth, creating an atmosphere both cozy and intimate.

The place was relatively empty at this hour, which suited our purposes. We ordered food, then leaned closer across the table.

"What's troubling you most?" Lex asked, her voice low.

"Too many directions, not enough concrete leads," I admitted. "The attempted hack into my system, the threats against you, Nightingale's behavior…"

"Each is connected to Labyrinth," she concurred.

"If the consortium knows we're investigating them, they'd try to disrupt our efforts on multiple fronts."

Her eyes brightened. "Exactly. They're trying to distract us, make us chase shadows while they advance their plans."

The arrival of our food—steak and ale pie for me, fish and chips for her—temporarily paused our conversation.

"I've been thinking about Edinburgh," she said eventually. "Orlov's work has always been extraordinary but fundamentally flawed from an ethical standpoint. He rejected all safeguards, arguing that true AI advancement required freedom from human constraints."

"Exactly the sort of philosophy Labyrinth would embrace," I said grimly.

Lex's response was cut short as a figure approached our table. To my surprise, it was Ambrose, looking unusually cheerful.

"Conrad! And Dr. Sterling, isn't it? What a delightful coincidence."

The man was as annoying as any I'd ever met, yet I greeted him cordially. "Ambrose. I didn't realize you frequented the Stag's Head."

"Oh, I've been coming here for decades." He waved at the barman, who immediately began pouring what was apparently his usual. "Mind if I join you? Just for a moment."

Before either of us could object, he slid into the booth, beside Lex, who shifted to accommodate him with a polite smile.

"I've just been in Tarbert, finalizing the acquisition of a rather remarkable painting for a client," he said, accepting his whiskey from the server with a grateful nod. "Sixteenth-century Flemish, believed lost during the war. Turned up in the estate of an elderly woman who had no idea of its value."

"How fascinating," Lex said, seeming genuinely interested. "You're an art dealer, then?"

"Among other things." Ambrose's eyes sparkled. "I specialize in locating the unfindable, connecting rare pieces with those who truly appreciate them."

I'd known Ambrose my entire life, and while he'd always been eccentric, today he seemed almost charming. He spoke animatedly with Lex about art history, displaying knowledge I hadn't realized he possessed.

"Evelyn was telling me about your work in AI," I heard him say. "Brilliant stuff, truly. She speaks very highly of you."

"Dr. McLaren has been a wonderful mentor," Lex replied. "She said you've been friends since university."

"That's right." He smiled fondly. "We're actually heading to a gallery opening in Glasgow this weekend. She has the most remarkable eye for detail—spots things most people miss entirely. Well, I'm off. Delightful seeing you again." He waved in my direction. "And you, Con."

After Ambrose left, promising to relay our regards to Dr. McLaren, Lex turned to me with raised eyebrows. "Is it my imagination, or do you think he fancies her?"

"God, I hope not." I shook my head, unable to reconcile the image. "I've never seen him that way with anyone. It's…unsettling."

"I found him endearing," she said, amusement dancing in her eyes.

"Brose is many things, but 'endearing' has never been one of them."

We finished our meal and settled the bill, both of us more relaxed than when we'd arrived. The walk back to my SUV took us through the village square, past stone cottages with smoke curling from chimneys.

"It's beautiful here," Lex said, her breath visible in the cold air. "Peaceful, despite everything."

"That's why I come back," I admitted. "Edinburgh, even London, has advantages, but this…" I gestured to the rolling hills beyond the village. "This grounds me."

Rather than returning to Blackmoor straightaway, I ventured south to Tarbert. Once there, I suggested we take the ferry over to the Isle of Arran.

"I'd love it," Lex said with a wide smile and sparkling eyes.

"You are so beautiful," I murmured, reaching out to touch her cheek. "Brilliant and beautiful."

Her cheeks flushed as she whispered her thanks.

In the confined space of the vehicle, I remained acutely aware of her presence—the subtly of her natural scent, the warmth radiating from her body, the rhythm of her breathing. Tensions of a different sort replaced our earlier concerns, building with each kilometer.

My mobile rang, and Gus' name flashed on the screen.

"Where are you?" he blurted when I put the call on speaker.

"About to get on the ferry to Arran."

"We've intercepted something. Unusual communications from a facility near Dundee. Similarly encrypted to what we tracked from the St. Petersburg connection."

"Give us forty-five minutes, and meet us at Blackmoor."

"Copy that. See you then."

I ended the call and looked over at her.

"We should head back," Lex said, her eyes boring into mine.

"We should do." I maneuvered my vehicle out of the ferry line. "Another time, though, yes?"

"I'd like that."

Back in the ops hub, Lex, Gus, and I huddled over the data he'd transmitted. The communications were heavily encoded, but certain things stood out.

"This section here." Lex pointed to a sequence on the screen. "The structure is distinct. It's Orlov's. I recognized it from a conference he presented at years ago."

"So he's in Scotland, not Russia?" I leaned closer, our shoulders touching.

"Not necessarily. But his work certainly is." She glanced at me, our faces unexpectedly close. "He could be directing this remotely."

For hours, the three of us worked side by side, breaking down the ciphered communications and forming hypotheses.

"I'd really like to have Dr. McLaren take a look at this."

My first reaction was to say no. However, recalling what she'd said earlier, I kept quiet.

"I'll ring her in the morning," she said, stifling a yawn.

"Time for me to go," said Gus, standing and stretching. "I'm famished."

"Apologies. I could have Mrs. Thorne make something."

"And have my mum get wind of it? No thanks," he joked.

We walked him upstairs, and after we'd said good night, I asked Lex if she was hungry too.

"Not really. I could go for a brandy, though."

We went into the library, falling into an easy conversation about what our parents' hopes and dreams were for us when we were young.

"The expectation was always that I'd take over Blackmoor, which I did do after my father passed. Just not in the way he imagined, I'm sure."

"What about your mum?" she asked.

"They divorced when I was at university. She remarried a bloke from the States. I don't see her often. What about you?"

"My father wanted me to study literature," she confessed with a soft laugh. "He was horrified when I chose computer science. 'Machines have no soul,' he told me. I've spent my career trying to prove him both right and wrong."

"How so?" I asked, genuinely curious.

"While he was right about the machines themselves, they reflect the souls of their creators," she said, her expression thoughtful. "That's why ethics in AI development matters so much. We're creating mirrors of ourselves, for better or worse."

"That's why Labyrinth terrifies me."

When the clock chimed twelve, I was stunned at how late it was. "We should get some rest," I said reluctantly.

"We should."

We made our way up the stairs and I was about to open her door when Lex's mobile chimed with an incoming message. Her face paled as she read it.

"What is it?" I asked, instantly alert.

She handed me the phone. The message was short but chilling.

Your room isn't as private as you think. They're watching. Listening. Trust no one at Blackmoor.

A cold fury rose in me, compounded by fatigue and frustration. Someone was deliberately trying to make her feel unsafe in my home. I removed my mobile and scanned the corridor for listening devices, then took her arm gently.

"Let me check your room," I said, my voice low but firm.

I entered and conducted a thorough sweep, checking for any type of intrusion. The search revealed nothing, which almost worried me more than finding something would have.

"It appears clean," I said, pocketing my mobile.

"That doesn't make the message any less disturbing," she replied, arms crossed protectively over her chest. For the first time since I'd met her, Lex looked genuinely rattled. The confident, challenging woman had momentarily given way to someone vulnerable.

"I don't think you should stay here tonight," I began, then immediately clarified when her eyebrows rose. "I mean in this room. There are other guest suites, or—"

"Or?"

The word hung between us as I stepped closer. "You could stay with me. Not here. In the west wing."

Her head cocked.

"It's where I usually sleep."

She looked up at me. "Usually?"

I motioned to the adjoining suite. "I wanted to remain close."

"Why?"

"I don't know. I just—" I couldn't say which of us moved first. One moment, we were standing apart. The next, my hands were in her hair and her arms were around my neck, our lips meeting in a kiss that sent scorching heat through my veins. Her body felt warm and solid against mine. Perfect, really.

When we finally broke apart, both breathing hard, she kept her hands on my shoulders as if steadying herself. I felt equally unbalanced, caught in a current I hadn't planned to navigate.

"That was…" she began.

"Yes," I agreed, knowing exactly what she meant. "Come with me."

I led her to the other side of the castle and into my suite. Unlike those upstairs, this entire wing was wired to detect any intrusion, including from electronic devices.

"I'll, uh, give you a few minutes to, err, get ready for bed."

She stepped closer and rested her hands on my chest. "You've never done this, have you?"

I raised a brow. "Well, ahem, perhaps a time or two…"

She smiled. "Not that. I mean, invite a woman into your bed just to sleep."

"You're probably right. Do you think you'll be able to? Sleep, I mean." I tucked a strand of hair behind her ear.

She leaned into my touch, her eyes closing briefly. "I don't know."

"Come," I said, leading her over to the bed. We lay on the mattress, her in my arms, removing only our shoes. And when I felt Lex's breathing even out, I allowed myself to sleep too.

The next time I opened my eyes, I was stunned to see light streaming in through the windows. More, that Lex was no longer beside me.

10

I eased out of Con's bed well before dawn, trying my best not to wake him. His breathing remained deep and steady, his face relaxed in sleep—a stark contrast to the guarded expression he typically wore. I watched him for a couple of minutes, memorizing his features.

What was I doing? I thought with a start. This wasn't me. Dr. Margot Sterling didn't moon over men like some lovesick teenager. I was MI6's foremost AI-weapons expert, not a woman who abandoned all professional boundaries for a handsome face and sharp intellect.

Yet, here I was.

With reluctance, I left his bedroom and navigated the castle's shadowy corridors to one of my favorite rooms—the library. The massive oak door opened silently on well-oiled hinges. Inside, embers still glowed in the fireplace, casting just enough light to see where I was going. Rather than switching on the lamps, I moved to the windows and opened the heavy curtains, allowing the predawn glow to filter in.

My intention had been to find something to read, to distract myself from the warmth of Con's body that I longed to snuggle against. Instead, I found myself drawn to the photographs arranged on various surfaces—Con as a child, as a teenager, always with the same expression. There was a certain twinkle in his startling blue eyes, as if he knew a great secret.

In one photo, he stood beside his three friends, all of them preteens, arm in arm before what appeared to be this castle. David's blond hair caught the sunlight, Tag's dark curls contrasted with Con's straighter locks, and Gus stood slightly apart, his smile more reserved than the others. Four boys with no idea they'd grow into men who would combat global threats.

Another photograph showed Con as a baby, cradled in a woman's arms—his mother, presumably. She had the same sapphire-blue eyes, her smile tentative as she looked down at her son.

I picked up a silver frame that held a picture of Con at perhaps sixteen, standing proudly beside what must have been his first car. His smile was genuine, unguarded in a way I hadn't witnessed until last night.

What would a life with Con Carnegie be like? The thought ambushed me, leaving me breathless. Would we split our time between London and Blackmoor? Would there be children who inherited his technological brilliance or my analytical approach?

The mental image of a dark-haired child with Con's eyes and my button nose made my heart constrict.

Good God—one night sleeping beside him, and I was imagining our hypothetical offspring?

"Planning to steal my baby pictures for blackmail?"

I nearly dropped the frame, spinning around to find Con leaning against the doorjamb arms crossed over his chest. He'd thrown on a T-shirt and flannel bottoms, his feet bare on the stone floor. His hair was tousled from sleep, and a stubbled shadow darkened his jaw. The combination was devastating.

"You caught me," I replied, setting the photo down. "I was negotiating with several tabloids for exclusive rights."

He chuckled, the sound low and warm as he crossed the room toward me. "Find anything particularly incriminating?"

"The photo with the car. Not exactly the imposing Earl of Blackmoor image you cultivate now."

"Ah, yes. My first vehicle—bought with money I made selling an algorithm I'd designed. My father was livid. He wanted me to focus on my studies, not 'dabble in computer nonsense,' as he put it."

Con stood close enough now that I could feel the heat radiating from his body. "I was disappointed to wake and find you gone."

My throat tightened at the quiet admission. "I needed to think."

"About the same thing I've been."

I smiled. "Reading my mind now?"

He brushed a strand of hair from my face, his fingertips lingering against my cheek. "Let's have breakfast. I'm famished."

The moment broke, and I followed him toward the morning room, trying to sort through my jumbled emotions. Last night had changed something fundamental between us. The tension remained, but it had transformed from adversarial to anticipatory. Each accidental touch as we walked side by side sent desire straight to my core.

Breakfast was set out the same way it had been every day since I arrived. As Con poured coffee, his eyes met mine over the rim of his cup.

"What are your plans for today?" he asked.

"I'd like to meet with Dr. McLaren if she's available."

"You should reach out to her. I expect she and Ambrose will be back from Stirling by now."

His easy agreement surprised me. "No objections this time?"

"You made your point yesterday. I respect your judgment." He spread marmalade on his toast, then licked some off his finger. The sight made me dizzy. God, how I wanted this man.

"Lex? Still with me?"

"Sorry, what? I was lost in thought for a moment."

"I said, if our suspicions about Orlov are correct, her insights could prove invaluable."

"Yes. Most definitely," I acknowledged, slathering marmalade on my toast like he had. When I turned around to join him at the table, he was standing right behind me.

"You're distracted," he said, taking my plate from my hand and setting it on the sideboard. "Anything you want to talk about?"

You. Me. Naked. Back in bed. I wondered how he'd react if I threw caution out the window and said it out loud. Sadly, for me to ever get up the nerve to, I'd have to have a complete personality transplant. "I, err, should probably message Dr. McLaren now." I skirted around him and out into the hall, where I leaned against the stone wall, hoping it would cool me off. Evelyn, not that I ever called her that, responded almost immediately, inviting me to join her at Ashcroft midafternoon.

"All set?" he asked when I returned and saw he'd moved my plate to the table where he sat.

"Yes. Ashcroft at fifteen hundred."

"I'd like to join you."

My eyes met his, and the challenge I saw in them previously was gone. "I'm sure Dr. McLaren wouldn't mind."

He reached for my hand after I took my seat. "What about you, Lex? Would you mind?" His thumb brushed the inside of my palm, making it impossible for me to think.

"I would not," I said, jerking it away with more force than I'd intended.

His eyes flared.

"Sorry, it's just…"

"Look, if you prefer I not, I'll respect your wishes."

"It isn't that, Con."

He stood to get more coffee. "What is it, then?"

"You."

"Me?"

"You make it hard for me to think at times," I admitted.

His scowl was quickly replaced by a wide smile.

I shook my head, unable to keep from grinning as well.

His hand reached for mine again. "You do the same to me, you know?"

After breakfast, we retreated to the ops hub, the professional setting a stark contrast to the scene of our breakfast flirtatiousness.

"The Russian we overheard mentioned a demonstration within the month," I said, typing notes as I spoke. "Which means—"

"They'd need to conduct the final integration testing within the next week," Con finished.

I continued typing. "And given what we know about his previous work, Orlov would need specialized hardware for that phase." An alert popped up on my screen. "What's this?" I asked.

Con leaned over my shoulder, his chest briefly pressing against my back. The contact, though fleeting, made me shiver in a way that had nothing to do with the temperature in the underground facility.

"I reached out to Sullivan to see if her sources were able to confirm shipments taking place in the next seven days. It appears she had success," he said before moving over to his workstation.

By early afternoon, we'd compiled a comprehensive analysis of potential locations for Labyrinth's operations, narrowing our focus to three specific areas within Scotland that had the infrastructure necessary for advanced AI-weapons development, as well as easy access to Teesport, where the previous shipments Sullivan had tracked departed from.

"Time to go," said Con.

I was stunned when I checked and saw it was already fourteen-thirty. "I'll just grab a coat."

"Ahem."

"Oh, you have it already," I said, turning to see it dangling from one of Con's fingers. I stood, and he helped me with it. Admittedly, I loved how much of a gentleman he could be when he decided he wanted to.

The drive to Ashcroft was under rain-heavy clouds that threatened but hadn't yet broken. The castle's silhouette against the darkening sky was imposing, particularly given it sat on a promontory.

"Dr. Sterling, how lovely to see you again. Lord Blackmoor," Mairi greeted us at the entrance with a warm smile. She gave a slight bow that seemed more habitual than necessary. "Dr. McLaren is waiting in the library. I'll bring tea shortly."

Following Mairi through Ashcroft's corridors, I noted the similarities and differences between this castle and Blackmoor. Both possessed the weight of history in their stone walls, but where Blackmoor felt like Con—controlled elegance with cutting-edge technology hidden beneath traditional surfaces—Ashcroft carried a more mysterious energy, secrets tucked away in shadowed corners.

We entered the library to find Dr. McLaren examining a leather-bound volume at a table near the windows. She looked up as we walked in, her eyes briefly registering surprise at Con's presence before her professional mask reasserted itself.

"Margot, Conrad, thank you for coming." She closed the book and gestured to the chairs across from her. As we settled, she continued, "A magnificent room, isn't it? Though I understand it has a troubled recent history."

"This is where Fallon Wallace abducted Sullivan Rivers," Con confirmed, his voice flat despite the personal nature of the statement. "She took her through a concealed entrance behind a bookcase that led to the tunnels beneath the estate."

Dr. McLaren's eyes widened slightly. "So the rumored passages are real. Fascinating from a historical perspective, though clearly dangerous in the wrong hands." She shifted her attention to me. "You mentioned concerns about Viktor Orlov?"

"First, whether or not he's alive."

"While I too have heard the rumors, I've not received confirmation that they're true."

"Acting on the supposition he is, would he be capable of developing a comprehensive AI-weapons system?"

Her eyebrows flashed. "Capable? I suppose so." For the next hour, Dr. McLaren proved why she'd been the foremost AI ethics expert in SIS, maybe even in all the world. Her knowledge of the neural network design was mind-boggling, and her analysis of Orlov's previous work incisive.

"As you know, Viktor was brilliant but entirely lacking a moral code," she explained, spreading diagrams across the table. "His approach to recursive learning algorithms was revolutionary, but he rejected the ethical constraints as 'limitations on evolution,' as he put it."

"Were you able to review the transcripts from Nightingale's interview?" I asked.

Dr. McLaren's expression grew serious. "I have done, and if Orlov—or someone else—is pursuing true autonomous integration, he's attempting something most researchers consider impossible." She shook her head. "The computational requirements alone would exceed most current hardware capabilities."

"But if he had access to specialized neural processors?" Con asked, leaning forward.

"Even then, full autonomy without human oversight mechanisms is a pipe dream." Her dismissal seemed confident, yet something in her expression gave me pause. "Besides, the ethical implications alone would prevent any major world power from deploying such a system."

"Fallon Wallace and Tower-Meridian weren't concerned with ethics," Con pointed out.

"No, they weren't," Dr. McLaren conceded. "But there's a vast difference between designing a weapon with limited autonomous capabilities and creating a truly independent system." She gathered her notes. "I'd be happy to review any technical specifications you uncover. Orlov's work was distinctive—I could identify his fingerprints if you find concrete examples."

By the time we concluded our meeting, the sky had darkened further, heavy clouds promising an imminent downpour. Con and I thanked Dr. McLaren and hurried toward his vehicle, making it barely halfway across the courtyard before the heavens opened.

The rain fell in sheets, instantly soaking through our clothing. Con grabbed my hand, and we ran the remaining distance, laughing despite—or perhaps because of—the absurdity of our situation. By the time we reached the SUV, we were both drenched, my blouse clinging to my skin even under my coat, his hair plastered to his forehead.

"The weather couldn't have held off for two more minutes?" He shook his hair as he started the engine.

"Clearly not," I replied, attempting to wring water from my sleeve with little success. "My laptop bag is waterproof, thank God, but the rest of me is a lost cause."

Con glanced over, his eyes darkening as they traced the outline of my body beneath the sodden cloth-ing. I met his gaze directly, and his eyebrows flashed like Dr. McLaren's had, although for an entirely different reason.

The drive back to Blackmoor seemed interminable, tension building with each kilometer. When we finally arrived, Con parked haphazardly near the entrance and we both emerged into the continuing downpour. Halfway to the door, he caught my hand, pulling me to a stop.

Rain streamed down his face as he looked at me, his blue eyes intense. Without a word, he leaned down and captured my lips with his. The kiss was hunger unleashed, his hands threading through my wet hair as mine gripped his shoulders.

When we broke apart, both breathing heavily, he rested his forehead against mine. "We should get out of these wet clothes," he suggested, his voice rough.

He led me inside but not to my suite. I followed him into his bedroom, where he opened a wardrobe and withdrew a thick robe in deep navy blue.

"Here," he said, handing it to me. "You can, err, change in the bathroom if you'd like."

I took the soft, luxurious robe, holding it close to my body as much for warmth as for anything else. An unbidden thought crossed my mind—who else had worn this? Had Fallon wrapped herself in this same fabric after sharing his bed?

As if reading my thoughts, Con cupped my cheek, his eyes meeting mine. "It's yours," he said softly. "No one else's."

The simplicity of his statement washed away my insecurity. I slipped into the bathroom, peeling off my wet clothing and drying myself with a plush towel before wrapping the robe around me.

When I emerged, the flames of the fire he'd lit cast flickering shadows across the room. From where he stood near the window, I saw he'd changed into dry trousers and a simple white shirt, its top buttons undone.

"I asked Mrs. Thorne to prepare a casual dinner," he said. "I hope you don't mind if we remain in here while we eat."

"Not at all."

We sat on the floor before the fire on cushions arranged in a makeshift dining area. Con poured us each a glass of wine, in what was quickly becoming the most romantic night of my life.

"What did you make of Dr. McLaren's assessment?" he asked, passing me a glass.

"Her dismissal of AIWS seemed too absolute," I admitted. "I'd say it wasn't like her, but it's one of the things we often disagreed about."

"I thought the same." He took a sip of wine, his eyes never leaving mine. "The question is why."

"Maybe she doesn't want to consider the worst-case scenario." I set my glass next to his on the hearth. "We should compile a list of potential—"

My words cut off as Con leaned forward and kissed me, gently at first, then with growing intensity. The discussion of Labyrinth faded to insignificance as his hands framed my face, his thumbs tracing my cheekbones.

"I can't count the number of times today I wanted to take you in my arms," he confessed against my lips.

"I wanted you to," I whispered back, my hands finding the buttons of his shirt.

We abandoned our dinner, wine forgotten as our clothing was discarded piece by piece. Con's body was a revelation—broad shoulders tapering to narrow hips, muscles defined but not excessive, the picture of a man who maintained his physical condition as meticulously as his technological expertise.

His hands found the belt of my robe, pausing at the knot. "Are you certain?" he asked, his voice husky.

In answer, I untied it myself, letting it fall open. His sharp intake of breath was gratifying, his eyes darkening as they traveled over me.

"You're extraordinary," he said, lowering me gently onto the blanket spread out on the floor.

What followed was exploration and discovery, his hands and mouth learning every curve and hollow of my body as mine mapped the contours of his.

"Lex—" Whereas before he'd asked directly, now he seemed to be waiting for me to speak first.

"I want to be with you, Con," I said, not wanting to waste time. We were both adults, lying naked side by side. Now was hardly the time to change our minds, not that I would've.

Rather than respond with words, he lifted me in his arms and carried me to the bed where I'd slept beside him.

"God, you're beautiful," he said, pulling a condom from the bedside drawer and eyeing me through heavy, dark lashes. "Everything about you…"

"Con, please." I reached for him, longing to feel his skin against mine again.

Setting the packet on the bed, he leaned forward, weighing the heavy flesh of my breasts with both hands. My need for him intensified when he brushed his thumbs over my hardened nipples.

"The scent of your desire is intoxicating," he said, bringing his mouth where his fingers were, then closing it around one nipple.

I gasped when the fingers of his other hand moved between my legs, pushing them open before cupping me.

"You're so wet." His voice was hoarse when his fingers penetrated me.

My body writhed. "I ache for you, Con."

"I cannot wait any longer." He tore the packet open, sheathed his hardness, then settled himself between my thighs. When he pressed against me, I knew my body would adjust and accept him, but I flinched nonetheless at his size.

"Do you trust me, Lex?"

My eyes met his. "I do."

"I won't hurt you." He eased the tip in just a little, then reached between us, finding my clit and toying with it until I nearly came.

I whimpered when he moved his hand away and eased his cock deeper at the same time he lowered his mouth and teased my breast before sucking it again. He let it go with a pop, then thrust hard inside me.

"We were made for this. You and me. A perfect fit."

His words melted me from the inside out, and tears filled my eyes. I pushed away the thoughts of him saying that to any other woman and focused on how right he was.

Con began to move, filling and stretching me, each stroke deliberate. I lifted my hips, meeting his thrusts, moving with him until we reached a frantic pace, pounding against each other. His fingers found my nub again, and with a cry, I shattered in his arms as though the pleasure was so intense that I'd break apart.

He held me, wrapping one arm under my arched back as he thrust again and again. His body stiffened, and he threw his head back, pressing deep inside me once more before I could feel him pulsing inside me as the rest of him stilled. He braced himself on his elbow, and our eyes met. The connection I felt then was so far beyond physical pleasure. The sensation of how right he was, how perfect we were together, was overwhelming.

When he eased himself from inside me, I whimpered again, this time at the emptiness I felt. He disposed of the condom, then gathered me in his arms, kissing me passionately as our hands renewed their exploration.

With the fire crackling near us, I traced circles on his chest, feeling the steady beat of his heart beneath my fingertips. Whatever complications tomorrow might bring—Labyrinth, Unit 23, the mysterious threats—in this moment, there was only Con and me, intertwined in the ember's glow.

I had no illusions that this solved anything. Our professional tensions would resurface. The threats surrounding us remained. But for now, in the sanctuary of his bedroom, I allowed myself to simply be a woman in the arms of a man who had somehow worked his way into my heart, something I couldn't bring myself to regret.

Con

Consciousness arrived like a gentle tide rather than by a jarring alarm that typically yanked me from sleep. I opened my eyes to find Lex curled against me, her dark hair spilling across my chest. The weight of her head resting over my heart created an unfamiliar sensation of…contentment.

I'd slept through the night. No nightmares about Fallon's betrayal, no waking in a cold sweat with fragments of failure echoing in my mind. Just uninterrupted rest with Lex in my arms.

My fingers traced the curve of her shoulder, marveling at the softness of her skin. Her brilliance had first captivated me, but this vulnerability—the trust required in our profession to sleep beside someone—moved me in ways I hadn't anticipated.

She stirred, eyelashes fluttering against her cheeks before opening. The moment of confusion in her eyes cleared, replaced by recognition and something warmer.

"Good morning," she said, voice husky with sleep.

"It is, indeed." I brushed a strand of hair from her face. "You're quite beautiful when you're saving the world in your dreams."

She laughed, the sound vibrating against my chest. "Who says I was dreaming?"

"Fair point." I shifted, pulling her closer. "I could grow accustomed to this."

"To what?" Her eyes held mine, searching.

"Waking with you. Sleeping through the night." I hesitated, then added, "Having someone who understands both sides of my life."

Her expression softened as she traced the line of my jaw with her fingertips. "I'm glad I stayed."

"As am I." I kissed her, marveling at how natural it felt. "Though I suspect Mrs. Thorne will have questions about our breakfast preferences."

She groaned, burying her face against my neck. "I hadn't thought about that. Your staff—"

"Are the soul of discretion," I assured her, though the thought of Bastion's raised brow made me wince internally. "Perhaps we should face the day."

In the shower, soap and water weren't our only considerations as hands wandered and lips met. What began as routine cleansing evolved into something far more intimate, leaving us both breathless, then fulfilled.

When we finally made our way downstairs, Mrs. Thorne had indeed adjusted the breakfast service. Two places were set side by side rather than across from each other at the table, and my coffee was stronger than usual. I couldn't speak for Lex's tea, but I assumed it was steeped extra long.

"Sleep well, my lord?" Bastion asked a few minutes later, his expression indiscernible as he refilled my coffee.

"Exceedingly, thank you." I caught Lex's eye over my cup, noting the hint of color in her cheeks.

After Bastion withdrew, she leaned toward me. "Does anything escape his notice?"

"Not in twenty years of service." I buttered a piece of toast. "Now, about today. We need to compile everything we have on Labyrinth's potential locations."

She reached for her tablet, professional focus returning. "The suspicious network traffic we identified yesterday should be our starting point."

We were debating approaches when my secure mobile vibrated with an encrypted message. Kestrel's identifier flashed on the screen as I opened it.

"Well, this is interesting." I passed her the device.

She read aloud. "A Russian scientist matching Orlov's description was seen working at a converted estate in Aberdeenshire. Defense measures in place, including signal jamming and thermal detection grids. Satellite imagery is attached." She looked up, eyes bright with the thrill of a solid lead. "This could be it."

I downloaded the attached files to review on a larger screen. "Aberdeenshire makes sense—remote enough for privacy but with port access."

"And close enough to the North Sea for a quick evacuation if necessary." She set down her cup. "We should examine those satellite images immediately."

Twenty minutes later, we were in my ops hub, Kestrel's images displayed across multiple screens. The estate was centered around what appeared to be a small, centuries-old castle—not unlike Blackmoor but more compact—with several newer structures dotting the perimeter. The original stonework stood in stark contrast to the modern additions.

"Look at this," Lex noted, indicating a series of regular points along the property boundary. "Those aren't standard cameras."

"Thermal and motion detection," I agreed. "Military grade, based on the spacing."

She moved closer to the screen, analyzing the layout. "The north wing of the castle has nonstandard power lines. Either they're running something that requires enormous energy—"

"Or they're maintaining a completely independent power system. Either way, it suggests advanced technical infrastructure."

"They wouldn't need much space for AIWS," she explained. "The beauty of neural networks is their computational density. A facility the size of one wing in a small castle could house everything necessary for Labyrinth's core systems." Lex took a step back and tapped her cheek. "We need to get eyes on this place, but drones would be detected immediately."

"Ground views, then." I pulled up topographical maps of the surrounding area. "There's elevated terrain to the northwest that would provide decent sight lines to the main facility."

As we developed our plan, I made a decision I'd never made before. Opening a secure terminal, I entered a series of commands, then turned to her.

"I'm giving you access to another network," I said, entering the final authorization codes. "Complete access, not just the sanitized version Unit 23 sees."

Her eyes widened. "Con, that's—"

"Necessary," I finished. "If we're going to stop Labyrinth, we need to pool resources."

She nodded, the significance of my gesture not lost on her. "Thank you. And in that spirit…" She retrieved her tablet and entered a complex sequence. "This is my research on neural-network architectures developed for military applications. It's classified beyond what I've given to Unit 23."

I scrolled through her data, impressed by both the technical depth and her willingness to share it.

"This will help identify Orlov's fingerprints if we find any systems at the estate," she added.

By midmorning, we had established a preliminary plan. I contacted Gus to run background checks on the estate and everyone connected to it. Before I did so, I asked about Nightingale. "Any update?"

"None whatsoever. To be honest, Con, I'm worried about Tag."

As was I, particularly since his admission that he and the missing operative were far more than colleagues.

"I've got a hit," he said after a few seconds of silence. "The property was purchased eleven months ago by Highlands Research Partners, which traces back to yet another shell company, Nova Perspectives."

Lex gasped. "The private think tank specializing in AI applications?"

"That's right," Gus confirmed.

"We should prepare for at least three days of continuous observation," I said after the call with him ended.

As we gathered the equipment, I showed Lex some of the modifications I'd made to the standard gear that reduced detection significantly.

"Is this a signal-masking device?" She held up a small black box I'd designed.

"It works on the principle that most systems look for disruptions, not absence," I explained, pleased by her appreciation of the technical nuance. "When Fallon was at Blackmoor—"

Lex stilled, her eyes meeting mine, the mood shifting instantly.

"I apologize," I said, tension tightening my shoulders. "I shouldn't bring her up."

"No, we need to be able to discuss her," she replied. "She was central to Labyrinth's development. Pretending otherwise compromises our investigation."

The understanding in her voice helped ease the knot in my throat. "She used my expertise, asking all the right questions to extract information."

"That's what made her dangerous," Lex said, eyes hardening. "Her ability to manipulate people without revealing her motives."

Later, as we finalized our preparations, I found myself sharing more than just professional strategies. We moved from my operations hub to the library, where the fire had been lit against the growing evening chill.

"My father thought technology was beneath our family's dignity," I said, sipping the whiskey I'd poured us. "The Earl of Blackmoor should concern himself with land management and tradition, not coding and systems."

"What about your mother?" Lex asked, tucked beside me on the sofa.

"She encouraged my interests, which only widened the gulf between them." I stared into the amber liquid in my glass. "Their marriage ended during my first year at Cambridge. He blamed her for my career choice."

"That's absurd," she said, indignation flaring in her voice.

"It was convenient. Their problems ran deeper." I set my glass down. "What about your family? You mentioned your father wanted you to study literature."

"He was an English professor. Believed computers would dehumanize education." She smiled faintly. "He and my mother had my whole life planned—I'd teach at a women's college, marry a colleague, and publish scholarly articles on Jane Austen."

"Instead, you're developing countermeasures for AI-weapons systems while bedding an earl with dubious business interests." I raised an eyebrow. "I imagine Christmas dinners are interesting."

Her expression changed. "Were. They both passed shortly after I graduated university."

"I'm sorry, Lex," I said, reaching for her hand.

"It's why Dr. McLaren is so important to me. It isn't like she stepped into the role of my mother or father, but she did take me under her wing, so to speak, enough that I pursued the career I wanted and had her support in doing so." She shook her head and blinked away the tears I was sure she'd not want me to see. "Change of subject?" she asked more than said.

"Come with me. There's something I want to show you."

I led her to a part of the castle few people ever saw—a small chamber off the main library, where the Carnegie family kept its most treasured historical items. Unlocking the heavy oak door with a key I kept hidden in a secret compartment, I ushered her inside.

"This is remarkable," she breathed, taking in the glass cases containing everything from medieval weapons to delicate jewelry.

I opened a drawer in an antique cabinet and removed a worn leather journal. "My ancestor Robert Carnegie kept this during the Jacobite rising."

Lex gasped. "This is extraordinary, Con."

"There's more." I retrieved a small wooden box from another cabinet. Inside, nestled on faded velvet, lay a silver brooch set with Scottish river pearls. "This belonged to Elizabeth Carnegie, who hid Jacobite soldiers in Blackmoor Castle."

When Lex looked from the brooch to me, I closed the distance between us, then brushed her lips with mine. The kiss began tenderly but deepened as my arms encircled her.

When we finally separated, breathless, she rested her forehead against mine. "Thank you for sharing this with me."

"You're the first person I have," I admitted, holding her close in the room where generations of my ancestors had kept their most valuable possessions.

We remained there long into the evening, exploring the collection and each other. With each story shared, each artifact examined, the walls I'd built around myself after Fallon's betrayal crumbled further.

Tomorrow, we'd travel to Aberdeenshire, hunting for concrete evidence of Labyrinth's operations.

But tonight, in this sanctuary of history and trust, we strengthened the bonds that would sustain us through whatever challenges awaited.

When we finally returned upstairs to the bed I already considered ours, I ravished her body in a way that I hoped conveyed my growing feelings for her. While I could've made love to her until dawn, her reminder of the day ahead of us convinced us both we needed rest.

12

Lex

The journey to Aberdeenshire in Con's Range Rover took four hours. We'd arrived as dusk fell and checked into a small inn under false identities—as a married couple, no less—our cover story for the three days we planned to stay here.

After dining at a pub next door, we returned to our room, making love until we fell into a contented sleep.

This morning, that feeling lingered, my body still humming from the pleasure he'd given me, but I knew that my focus had to shift to our mission. We were here to gather evidence on Viktor Orlov, confirm his connection to Project Labyrinth, and figure out how to stop his progress in developing AIWS.

"Based on the satellite imagery, the estate sits approximately three kilometers north of this position," Con said, pointing to a topographical map spread across the table in our room. "We'll approach on foot through the forest on the west. The elevation here"—he traced a ridge line with his finger—"should provide ideal sight lines to the main compound without exposing our presence."

I studied the terrain. "Their thermal detection grid has blind spots if we stay within the trees until this point." I indicated a position where the forest extended closest to the compound.

We parked the vehicle on an old logging road and covered it with a camouflage tarp. Con shouldered a backpack containing our equipment while I carried another with supplies we might need for an extended observation. Despite the seriousness of our mission, I couldn't help but admire his obvious comfort in field operations—a side of him I hadn't witnessed before.

The trek through the dense Scottish woods took almost an hour. Con moved ahead of me with the silent grace of someone well practiced in covert approaches. Following his lead, I matched his footfalls, mindful not to disturb the underbrush.

When we reached the ridgeline, Con raised his hand to signal a halt and activated our signal-masking device before we moved to the observation point.

From our elevated position, we had a much better view of the estate than the satellite imagery had provided.

Con unpacked a high-powered spotting scope while I assembled a digital camera with a telephoto lens. We worked in companionable silence, our movements synchronized as if we'd done this dozens of times together.

"I count eight external cameras," I said through the comms. "Plus what appears to be motion sensors at two-meter intervals along the fence line."

We settled in for a long-term stakeout, documenting everything we saw in meticulous detail. As the day progressed, we made a record of the deliveries and staff rotations. The estate operated with military precision, hinting that whoever ran the facility had a background in safeguarding sensitive installations.

Late in the afternoon, a sleek black sedan with tinted windows approached the main gate. Unlike the previous vehicles, this one wasn't searched or delayed. The gates opened immediately, suggesting someone of importance had arrived.

"Get ready," Con whispered.

I focused my camera on the sedan as it pulled up to the main entrance. The rear door opened, and a tall, gaunt man emerged.

My breath caught. Though I could only see his profile, the distinctive way he moved was unmistakable—the slightly jerky gait, the rigid posture. I'd observed those same movements at three different AI conferences years ago.

"That's Orlov," I confirmed, snapping multiple photos.

Con's expression hardened. "Not a ghost, after all."

We continued our watch until dusk approached, capturing evidence of activity consistent with our suspicions. Through windows on the northern wing, I glimpsed what could be a testing facility—banks of computers, specialized equipment, and workstations arranged in a configuration I recognized from theoretical research.

"They're proceeding with integration trials."

"How far along would you estimate they are?" Con asked, his eyes never leaving the compound.

"Days from functional capability, not weeks."

Con's expression darkened. "We should head back. We've gathered enough for now, and I don't want to risk discovery."

The return journey was faster but more demanding as darkness fell. Con led us through the forest with unerring accuracy. However, by the time we reached the vehicle, my muscles ached from the day's exertion. I dozed off more than once on the return trip to the inn.

Rather than retiring to bed when we arrived, we set up our equipment, converting the room into a temporary ops center. Neither of us mentioned sleep; we both knew the evidence we'd gathered needed immediate analysis.

"Let's return later tomorrow," Con said as we worked. "I want to observe their night operations and document any additional deliveries. We still have two more days booked here."

"Roger that," I said, connecting my camera to one of his secure terminals. "I'll also start processing the images we captured."

"And I'll cross-reference what we've seen with known shipments of quantum-computing equipment."

For the next two hours, we worked side by side, compiling and analyzing everything we'd documented. The energy between us had shifted from the intimacy of the previous night to the focused intensity of two operatives in a race against time.

"Look at this," I said, pointing to enhanced images of the facility's northern wing.

Con leaned closer, his shoulder brushing mine. "They've installed a dedicated power infrastructure. That level of energy consumption suggests…"

"Neural processing on a massive scale," I finished. "Consistent with a fully autonomous system."

We spent the next two days the same way, documenting everything down to the most minute detail, then analyzing our findings each evening. By the third day, we had amassed substantial evidence of Labyrinth's development, along with an absolute certainty Orlov was implementing a truly autonomous AI-weapons system, the implications of which were catastrophic.

We packed up early on our final day, both concerned about ruining our cover by hanging around any longer. The return journey to Blackmoor was long but gave us time to discuss our findings and formulate the next steps.

It was late evening when we finally arrived at the gates of Blackmoor. Despite our exhaustion, we went directly to Con's ops hub to upload and secure our evidence.

As we compiled our findings into a secure file, Con's encrypted communication system alerted us to an incoming message. His expression darkened as he read it.

"What is it?" I asked, moving to his side.

"I received word from one of my sources in London. There's unusual activity at a facility in Canary Wharf consistent with what we observed in Aberdeenshire."

"Labyrinth has a lab in London?" My pulse quickened. "That's significantly more concerning than a remote Scottish location."

Con was already typing rapid commands. "I need to mobilize resources immediately. I have contacts in London who can get in place without drawing attention."

I watched as he accessed private channels, dispatching instructions to operatives I hadn't known existed. He worked with the confidence of someone accustomed to commanding resources outside official channels.

"We should coordinate with my MI6 team," I suggested, reaching for my secure mobile. "Viper has assets throughout London who could supplement your network."

"No," he said, not even raising his head.

I stared at him. "No?"

"We can't risk it." His voice was firm, brooking no argument. "MI6 would require documentation, approval chains, and resource allocation requests. We'd lose crucial hours, possibly days."

My mouth gaped. "My teams operate with the same urgency yours do."

"As you're abundantly aware, you don't have the same flexibility." His eyes never left his monitors. "My network can be in position within the hour, no questions asked, no paper trail."

I was stunned. "You can't be serious."

His eyes met mine for the first time in several minutes. "This is Unit 23 territory, Lex."

"To my knowledge, we haven't yet determined the need for an assassin."

He stood up straight. "As you also know, we do a fuck of a lot more than that."

"As does MI6. What's this about?" I asked, my voice sharpening. "Because it seems like you're making unilateral decisions about a joint operation."

He resumed typing. "This is about doing what works. Official channels have failed repeatedly in tracking Labyrinth—that's why we're in this situation, to begin with."

"And your private methods have been so successful?" I challenged. "From what I recall reading in the brief, Sullivan Rivers came damned close to losing her life."

Con went still, his fingers hovering over the keyboard.

"I apologized for that comment at Glenshadow," I said quickly. "I shouldn't have brought it up again."

"You meant it then, and you mean it now." His voice was cold. "The question is whether your loyalty to MI6 might similarly compromise our effectiveness."

Any regret I felt dissipated. "You're questioning my judgment? My professional competence?"

"I'm questioning whether you can operate beyond institutional constraints when necessary."

"That's rich, coming from a man whose entire operation exists outside accountability." I gestured to the underground facility around us. "You've built your own private intelligence agency, answerable to no one."

"It gets results," he said flatly.

"So does MI6, when given the chance." I stepped back, creating a physical distance that matched the emotional chasm opening between us. "I thought we were partners in this, Con."

"We are," he insisted, though his attention had already returned to the screens. "But sometimes, partnerships require one person to take the lead."

"And that person is always you?" I laughed without humor. "That's not a partnership—it's a subordinate relationship."

His blue eyes were hard when they bored into mine. "What would you suggest? That we waste precious time debating every decision? Lives are at stake, Lex."

"Don't patronize me. I'm well aware of the risks." I felt heat rising in my cheeks. "I've dedicated my career to stopping threats like this."

"Then, you should understand why rapid response matters more than procedural niceties."

"This isn't about procedures." My voice rose despite my efforts to control it. "It's about respect. You don't respect my expertise or my resources enough to fully integrate them with yours."

"That's not true," he said, but his tone lacked conviction.

"It is true. You see me as an MI6 representative first and a partner second." The realization struck me with painful clarity. "Even after everything."

Con ran a hand through his hair in frustration. "You're misinterpreting my concerns."

"Am I? Then, prove it. Let's develop a coordinated approach using both units."

He gestured to the incoming data stream. "My people are already moving into position."

I looked at him—really looked at him—and saw something I'd missed before. Behind his confident exterior was a man who couldn't relinquish control, who didn't truly trust anyone else's methods but his own. Not even mine.

"I see." I stepped away from the workstation. "When you invited me into your bed, did you think that meant I'd stop being your equal? That I'd simply defer to your judgment on everything?"

His expression hardened. "That's unfair."

"Is it?"

"Yes," he repeated.

"Prove it," I repeated.

His jaw tightened. "I've shared resources with you that no outsider has ever seen."

"Outsider." The word hung between us.

Con looked away, his silence more damning than any argument he could have made.

I reached for my mobile. "I'm returning to London."

"Lex—"

"No." I held up my hand. "When you're ready to work as the team we were assigned to be, you know where to find me. Until then, I'll pursue this investigation on my own."

I made the call as I returned to the main level of the castle, knowing he wasn't far behind. "Viper? It's Lex. I need transport back to London." I paused, listening to her response. "Yes, immediately."

Con followed me to my room, arguing his position the entire way. I changed into the clothes I'd arrived in, leaving everything else behind. Each item represented a connection to Blackmoor—to Con—that I couldn't bear to take with me.

"This is a mistake," he said from the doorway as I zipped my bag. "We don't have time for this," he said again, frustration evident in every line of his body.

I shouldered my bag. "I don't work this way. Not even with you."

The last thing I saw as the car Viper sent pulled away was Con standing alone on the steps of his ancestral home, a solitary figure against the ancient stone. The image stayed with me long after Blackmoor disappeared from view, a reminder of what might have been if only he could learn to share more than his bed.

13

Con

The wind bit through my jacket as I stood, staring at the empty driveway, rooted to the steps as if my presence might somehow reverse time and bring her back.

When the cold finally drove me inside, I headed straight to my ops hub, hoping work would distract me from the hollow space she'd left behind.

I kept replaying our argument, dissecting each word. She was right about one thing—I hadn't treated her as an equal partner. Yet I couldn't shake my conviction that my approach to Labyrinth was correct. Time wasn't a luxury we could afford with a threat of this magnitude.

My secure mobile buzzed with a message from one of my London operatives.

Unusual activity at Canary Wharf location. Equipment arriving via Thames shipping route. Being staged for immediate outbound shipment. Destination unknown.

I forwarded the message to Gus, then pulled up recent overhead footage of the Aberdeenshire estate. What I saw confirmed my growing unease—the site was bustling with unusual activity, vehicle convoys leaving the compound, and external power boosters being disassembled. The compound was clearly being abandoned.

"Bloody hell," I spat, typing commands to pull up the transportation records for the surrounding area.

The data told a story. Multiple freight vehicles had departed the Aberdeenshire location over the past twelve hours, their routes diverging. While some headed south, toward London, others pointed north on the A96. Cross-referencing it with the London reports suggested a complex operation—equipment being rerouted through multiple channels to mask the ultimate destination.

The timing was too perfect. Our observation had somehow compromised the site, forcing the consortium to relocate. Unless they were deliberately creating confusion, splitting shipments between multiple locations to obscure their true center of operations, the diverging transportation routes suggested a more sophisticated plan than a simple consolidation.

I raked my fingers through my hair, keenly aware of the empty chair beside me, where Lex should have been. We would have bounced theories off each other, her analytical mind complementing my instincts in a way I'd never experienced with anyone else.

My private channel pinged—Kestrel requesting connection. I encrypted the line and accepted.

"Your visit stirred the hornets' nest," Kestrel stated.

"They're relocating equipment from Aberdeenshire while also staging through London," I replied, skipping the pleasantries. "Any word on the final destination?"

"That's not my primary concern at the moment." The voice modulator couldn't mask the tension in his tone. "My sources are suggesting Russian handlers are putting extraordinary pressure on Orlov to accelerate testing."

My fingers stilled on the keyboard. "Why now?"

"A key component is failing—something in the neural interface. Unable to get anything more specific, but Orlov is pushing back, claiming he needs more time."

"And they're refusing to give it to him," I concluded. "Hence the rushed relocation."

"Yes, but there's more." Kestrel paused. "I've picked up chatter about a high-ranking AI-weapons specialist working with SIS being targeted."

Ice flooded my veins. "Targeted how?"

"Unclear. Could be for elimination or acquisition. The terminology was ambiguous."

But there was nothing ambiguous about who they meant. Lex was one of only three AI-weapons specialists at her level in SIS, and the only one actively investigating Labyrinth.

"Time frame?" I asked, already calculating how quickly I could reach London.

"Imminent. Within twenty-four hours."

After ending the call, I tried phoning Lex, but when it went to voicemail, I sent a text warning her of an urgent threat and to contact me immediately.

I slammed my fist against the desk. My priority should have been protecting her, not driving her away with my stubbornness. Now, she was in London, vulnerable and unaware she was being targeted.

"Bastion," I called, hitting the intercom. "Prepare the helicopter. I'm flying to London within the hour."

"Very good, sir. Shall I contact Mr. MacTaggert and Mr. Drummond as well?"

"Negative."

While gathering my essentials, my mind raced through the scenarios, none of them comforting. If the consortium believed Lex possessed information that could derail their plans, they wouldn't hesitate to eliminate her. If they valued her expertise and thought she could identify the reason for the interface failing, abduction was equally plausible.

Either way, I needed to reach her before they did.

On the way to my helicopter, I kept trying her mobile, each unanswered call increasing my anxiety.

At the airfield, I transferred directly to my waiting jet, barely acknowledging the ground crew. Aboard, I paced the cabin like a caged animal. Mrs. Thorne had packed a small bag for me, including a garment bag with formal wear I hadn't requested. The attached note simply read: "For when you apologize properly."

The woman knew me too well.

As the plane climbed through the cloud cover, I pulled out my mobile and dialed Viper's direct line. She answered on the second ring.

"Infidel," she greeted. "I wondered when I'd hear from you."

"Where is she?" I demanded, dispensing with the niceties.

"I don't believe Lex would approve of my sharing her location with you."

I closed my eyes, counting to five before responding. "Bellamy, I've received credible intelligence that Lex is being targeted by the consortium."

A pause followed. "How credible?"

"Kestrel."

"I see." Her tone shifted to business. "She's here at VX."

"I'm landing at Biggin Hill in ninety minutes. I'd like to speak with her."

"That's not my decision to make." Her voice cooled. "She'd throttle me for saying this, but you hurt her, Conrad. Not just professionally."

The accusation stung more than I'd expected. "I know."

"Do you? Because from what she's told me, you've demonstrated a remarkable talent for keeping people at arm's length while simultaneously drawing them into your orbit. It's quite a gift."

"I was wrong," I confessed, the words unfamiliar on my tongue. "About many things."

Viper sighed. "I'll tell her you're coming. The rest is up to her."

After the call ended, I stared out the window at the clouds below, contemplating the mess I'd made. My father had been exactly the same—brilliant, driven, utterly convinced of his own correctness. It had cost him his marriage and relationship with me. Now, I was repeating his mistakes, driving away the one person who understood both sides of my life.

My private mobile buzzed with a message from Tag.

Picked up Scottish police chatter. Gunfight reported at estate near Aberdeenshire. One casualty. Russian national, believed to be security personnel. No sign of Orlov.

I read the message twice, my pulse quickening. A security breach severe enough to result in casualties would explain the frantic relocation. The consortium would be moving Orlov and his work to safety. If rival interests were making bold moves, it made Lex's knowledge exponentially more valuable—and her danger more acute.

I rang Tag rather than messaging. "Send everything you have on the Aberdeenshire incident to my protected network. And contact Ash—I want firsthand observations from the scene ASAP."

"Already done. Gus is examining the shipping manifests from London ports. Equipment matching what we observed is being loaded onto a vessel registered to yet another shell company."

"Keep me updated." I ended the call and leaned back in my seat, pinching the bridge of my nose.

The pilot's voice came through the cabin speakers, informing me we'd encountered unexpected air traffic at Heathrow, requiring us to circle. We'd be delayed approximately thirty minutes.

I nearly put my fist through the bulkhead.

Unable to reach Lex directly and trapped in a metal tube, thousands of feet above ground, I did something I rarely allowed myself—I acknowledged I was afraid. Not just for her safety, but that I'd destroyed something irreplaceable before it had truly begun.

My fingers found the small object in my pocket—the silver brooch with Scottish river pearls I'd shown Lex in the family archive room. I'd grabbed it on impulse before leaving, thinking it might serve as a peace offering. Now, it felt like a talisman, connecting me to what mattered most.

Elizabeth Carnegie had worn this while protecting Jacobite soldiers. She'd done so because she believed in the cause, regardless of the risk. It struck me that Lex possessed that same courage—the willingness to stand her ground, even against me, when principles were at stake.

As the plane began its descent toward London, I made myself a promise. If—when—I reached Lex, I would lay my pride aside. For once in my life, I'd put someone else's opinions before my own, not because it was expedient, but because I trusted her judgment. Because I respected her as my equal.

Because I was falling in love with her.

The realization hit me with unexpected force. This wasn't mere attraction or professional admiration. Somehow, amid the danger and discovery, Lex had slipped past the barriers I'd maintained all my life.

I needed to tell her. If I wasn't too late.

The moment the wheels touched the tarmac, I checked my mobile. Nothing yet from Lex. However, a message from Viper provided an address—not MI6 headquarters, but a safe house in a Notting Hill mews.

I sent a brief reply. *On my way.*

As the plane taxied to a halt, I gathered my things, checked my weapon, and prepared to face whatever awaited me in London. Whether Lex would forgive me remained uncertain, but one thing was clear—I would do whatever necessary to keep her safe. Not just now, but for the rest of our lives if she'd let me.

14

Lex

While comfortable, the safe house in Notting Hill felt like a cage. After the sprawling grandeur of Blackmoor, the compact efficiency of MI6's London accommodation did little to settle my restless thoughts. My mobile sat on the table, its screen showing multiple missed calls and messages from Con. I hadn't answered any of them, needing space to sort through my tangled emotions.

I couldn't ignore them any longer. We were in the midst of an investigation that could result in a third world war; childish pride had no place here.

I scrolled through his messages. Each one grew progressively more urgent.

Need to talk. Important information about Labyrinth.

Please make contact when you get this.

Credible threat against you. Urgent you make contact immediately.

The last message had come through just before my signal disappeared entirely, which meant my window for responding was closed until MI6 tech support secured another communications channel.

The landline rang, startling me. Few people had that number.

"Sterling," I answered.

"Lex," Viper's voice came through. "Carnegie contacted me. He believes you're being targeted by the consortium."

"Who's his source?" I asked.

"Kestrel."

The name gave me pause. Even I knew his reliability was unquestionable.

"Con is flying in from Scotland. Should land within the hour," she continued. "I've authorized his access to the safe house. You can expect him shortly."

My heart did a traitorous little flip. "Thank you for the heads-up."

"In the meantime, you should know we've picked up unusual activity at Canary Wharf. Equipment arriving via Thames shipping routes, being prepared for immediate outbound transport."

"To Aberdeenshire?"

"Negative. We've also received reports indicating that compound has been abandoned. The timing suggests they're using London as a transit point. Final destination unknown."

After ending the call, I began tracing possible shipment origins, transit routes, and destinations on a digital map. Most appeared random at first glance, but several were scheduled to arrive at London ports within hours of each other, despite originating from different locations.

My mobile buzzed again with a message from Malcolm Bennett, the SIS agent who specialized in Russian counterintelligence and who Viper had recommended join the investigation, reiterating a death had occurred during the op.

I sat back, processing whether something else was at play here. Did the Russian national's death mean another entity had tried to take control over the AWIS development? If so, the list of who would was endless and wouldn't be limited only to those who wanted it to advance.

A subtle alert appeared on my tablet—a notification that someone with authorized credentials was approaching the safe house perimeter. A glance confirmed it was Con who, given Viper's estimated ETA, had made remarkably good time from the airfield. Still, safety protocols could not be ignored. I readied my weapon and got into position.

The subtle whir of the security system indicated someone had entered their access credentials. Moments later, the front door opened and closed with barely a sound. I kept my gun ready, moving silently toward the entrance hall.

"Lex?" Con's voice was low, controlled.

I lowered my weapon as he appeared in the doorway. The sight of him—dark hair disheveled by the wind, jaw set with determination, those piercing blue eyes— sent an unwelcome rush of emotions through me.

"You look like hell," I said, noting the shadows beneath his eyes.

"Hours without sleep will do that." He stepped closer and cupped my cheek. "Being terrified for your safety didn't help." He lowered his hand and motioned to a window. "Your team identified intruders. One in the back garden, eastern corner. Two more across the street." He moved to look, careful to stay out of sight. "They're not alone. I spotted two more on my approach. A five-person team suggests they're here for extraction rather than elimination."

"Con, I—" An alert on his mobile stopped me mid thought.

"We should relocate to the safe room," he said, glancing at the screen.

"Copy that."

We moved silently through the house to what appeared to be a coat closet in the hallway. I pressed my palm against a hidden scanner, revealing a reinforced door that led to a small, windowless room equipped with independent communications and defensive capabilities.

Once inside, I activated the secure systems while Con observed the external cameras.

"They're closing in," he reported as figures moved toward the house from multiple directions. "Professional team, coordinated approach. MI6 is authorized to take them out if necessary."

I leaned against the wall when adrenaline flooded my system.

"I shouldn't have let you leave Blackmoor alone," he said, moving away from the monitors and over to me.

"That wasn't your decision to make," I said with arms folded across my chest.

"No, it wasn't." His admission surprised me. "I was wrong, Lex."

I studied him, seeing genuine regret in his expression. "We're past that now. We need to focus on the present situation."

"The present situation includes us," he insisted. "When Kestrel told me you were targeted, I realized something I've been fighting against since we met." He was close enough for me to see the subtle flecks of darker blue in his eyes. "I need you. Not just for this mission. For everything."

My breath caught at the naked honesty in his voice. "Con—"

"Let me finish. Please." His tone had the rough edge of barely contained emotion. "I spent the entire flight to London thinking I might be too late. That I might never get the chance"—he exhaled slowly—"To tell you that I'm falling in love with you."

The world seemed to still around us. I had imagined many scenarios for our reunion, but this raw confession wasn't among them.

"You don't need to say that," I whispered.

"I do." His eyes remained steady. "Because it's true. And because life is too short and too uncertain to leave important things unsaid."

He reached into his pocket and withdrew something small. In his palm rested the silver brooch set with Scottish river pearls he'd shown me at Blackmoor.

"Elizabeth Carnegie's brooch," I breathed, recognizing it immediately.

"She wore this while protecting those she believed in, regardless of the personal risk." He held it out to me. "I want you to have it. Not as a peace offering, but because when I think of courage and principles, I think of you."

The gesture overwhelmed me. The brooch wasn't just a priceless family heirloom—it represented generations of Carnegie history. That he would entrust it to me spoke volumes. "I can't accept this," I said, though my fingers itched to touch it.

"You can," he insisted. "It's mine to give, and I choose you."

My hand trembled as I took the brooch, feeling its weight and history in my palm. "Thank you."

Despite the danger surrounding us, I felt something profound shift between us.

We remained in the small room until the "threat neutralized" message came from the team outside. Whether that meant they'd been taken out or apprehended didn't matter to me. Con did.

"I want to return to Blackmoor," I blurted.

He looked at me intently. "When?"

"As soon as possible. Now." My voice sounded frantic but not for reasons that made sense. Instead, it was about us. I needed to be as close to him as two people could be, and I didn't want it to be here, in a sterile safe house.

"Lex…what's going on?"

When I turned away from him, he wrapped his arms around me from behind and rested his chin on my shoulder.

"Don't shut me out. Talk to me," he implored.

"I don't want this…here."

Con gave a slight nod. "I have somewhere in mind for tonight. You'll be safe there. It's as secure as we'd be at Blackmoor."

"I don't care about that."

Con turned me in his arms and brushed my lips with his. "But I do, my sweet."

I shook my head. "It's okay. We can stay here."

"Lex, when we made love the first time, I asked if you trusted me."

"I do, Con, and I'm sorry that I didn't—"

He pressed a fingertip against my lips. "Trust me now."

"Okay," I whispered, resting my head against his chest. "Thank you for coming."

He lifted my chin. "Wherever you are, whatever you need, you can always count on me, Lex. Always."

"I believe you."

He kissed me again, then rested his forehead against mine. "That means more to me than you could know. Your trust, your belief in me. It's everything."

"I'm so sorry I doubted you."

"You were right to. It was the metaphoric kick in the arse I needed." He glanced over his shoulder. "Let's confirm we can get out of here, then I'll arrange transport."

Ten minutes later, an SUV with blackened windows pulled up directly in front of the mews. We exited through the same door Con had come in, and in two steps, were inside the secured vehicle.

"Courtesy of MI6," he said, shutting the armored door behind us. "Viper was quick to point out it wasn't my safety she was concerned with."

"Wait, why are we at Vauxhall Cross?" I asked when we pulled into the underground car park.

"It's a way station of sorts. When I asked for rooftop access, your boss requested a meeting prior to our return to Scotland."

We took the lift to the sixth floor, where Viper was waiting when the doors opened. "I'd ask how your morning went, but I've already been brought up to speed."

"I haven't," I told her.

She looked from me to Con.

"I have not been, either," he told her.

"Identified as Bratva associates. Which is one reason I requested Malcolm Bennett meet with us this morning. Admittedly, Dr. McLaren is annoyed to not have you to herself, not that she would've anyway. Although somehow, I don't think Con counts."

"Many thanks for that reassurance," he muttered under his breath.

We followed Viper down a corridor to one of the secure conference rooms. Malcolm Bennett stood when we entered, his imposing height emphasized by his ramrod-straight posture. Next to him, Dr. McLaren sat reviewing documents.

"Dr. Sterling, Lord Blackmoor." Bennett greeted us with a slight bow. "I understand you had an eventful morning."

"What do we know about the Bratva's involvement?" Con asked, cutting to the chase.

Bennett gestured to the digital display. "The men who attempted to abduct Dr. Sterling have direct ties to known Russian mafia operations in London and St. Petersburg."

"Are you certain it was a planned abduction?" I asked.

"I am," Bennett confirmed.

"Why me specifically?"

"I believe they weren't acting independently," Bennett replied. "They were contracted by someone with intimate knowledge of Project Labyrinth who needs your expertise."

Dr. McLaren looked up from her documents. "The Orlov connection would explain Bratva involvement. Viktor always maintained connections to elements in

Russia that walked the line between state-sanctioned and criminal enterprises."

"Including his brother," I added.

Dr. McLaren's eyes scrunched.

"You're aware of his connection to *Oruzhiye*, are you not?" Con asked.

"Of course," she muttered.

I glanced at Con, who'd clearly picked up on her lie the same as I had.

Bennett continued, "Orlov is likely encountering technical difficulties. Your expertise would be invaluable to solving their problems."

"That aligns with Kestrel's intelligence," Con added. "Russian handlers are pressuring Orlov to accelerate testing due to a failing component."

"What do you make of the facility relocation?" Viper asked.

Bennett spread surveillance photographs across the table. "The Aberdeenshire incident appears to be a coordinated extraction. One Russian security operative was killed, but I suspect it was deliberately staged."

"Staged?" Con and I asked simultaneously.

"The timing is too convenient. An attack occurs, creating a cover for abandoning the site at the same time equipment is already being routed through London," Bennett explained. "It's not a retreat—it's a planned consolidation."

"I agree," Dr. McLaren interjected. "They're making a critical transition in the development process. Orlov would need specialized equipment at this stage." She moved to the digital display. "This limits the potential relocation sites considerably. You need significant power infrastructure, specialized cooling capabilities, and physical isolation."

"Do you have a theory on the destination?" I asked.

"Given the shipping patterns and requirements, I believe they're moving to a coastal area with access to international waters."

Her finger stopped on Scotland's northern coast. "The former Naval Research Facility at Dunwich Bay would be ideal. It was decommissioned five years ago, but maintains the power-grid connections Orlov would require. More importantly, it has submarine access tunnels that would allow for rapid equipment transportation or evacuation."

"Submarine access?" Con asked. "That would explain the disjointed shipping routes—they're deliberately obscuring the final destination."

Bennett agreed grimly. "The facility at Dunwich Bay was sold to a private research consortium three years ago. I suspect we'll find connections to one of the shell companies identified in the Labyrinth investigation."

"If Dr. McLaren is correct," Viper said, "we have an extremely narrow window to intercept before the equipment and Orlov are secured."

"There's something else," Dr. McLaren added, her expression growing serious. "At this stage of the development, they're likely preparing for a practical demonstration."

"What kind of demonstration?" Con asked.

"The kind that would prove they've achieved true autonomous functionality," she replied. "Given Orlov's methodology, it would be something sufficiently dramatic to silence his critics and satisfy his backers."

The implication hung heavy in the room. This wouldn't be a theoretical exercise or limited field test, but a demonstration of the system's lethal potential.

"We need to move now," I said. "If they're consolidating at Dunwich Bay, we may only have days before they attempt whatever demonstration they're planning."

Bennett gathered his documents. "I'll dispatch surveillance teams to monitor their shipping activities. We should have confirmation within hours."

"In the meantime," Viper said, "proceed to your secure location as planned. Once we have confirmation, we'll coordinate a response."

Dr. McLaren approached me as the meeting ended. "Margot, a word?" Con stepped away to confer with Bennett.

"What is it?" I asked.

"Be careful," she said, her voice lowered. "Orlov's work has always pushed ethical boundaries, but what I've seen in the intercepts suggests he's gone beyond even his previous positions. Whatever they're building now…" She hesitated. "It may be more dangerous than anyone suspects."

"I'll keep that in mind," I promised.

"And Margot? Trust your instincts. They've always been your greatest strength."

I gave her a reassuring smile, somewhat puzzled by her emphasis but appreciative, nonetheless.

Con rejoined me. "Ready?" he asked quietly, his hand finding the small of my back.

As we exited Vauxhall Cross and headed toward the waiting helicopter, I couldn't shake the feeling that we were racing against something far more dangerous than just time. The consortium wasn't simply relocating their operations—they were preparing to demonstrate Labyrinth's capabilities in a way that would change everything.

And somehow, I knew we were central to whatever they were planning.

15

Con

I guided Lex from the lift as it opened directly into the marble foyer of my London residence. The soft whoosh of the doors closing behind us seemed to seal us away from the chaos we'd left at Vauxhall Cross.

"Welcome to what my staff insists on calling 'Sky Sanctuary,'" I said, pressing my palm against the biometric panel to deactivate the secondary security protocols. "Though I typically refer to it simply as the London flat."

She stepped farther into the entryway, surveying the sleek lines and modern aesthetic—a stark contrast to Blackmoor's ancient stones and historical weight.

"This is a flat?" Lex asked, one brow raised as she took in the expansive space before her.

I grinned at her reaction. "Perhaps I should have mentioned it spans the top three floors of One Hyde Park."

I watched her expression change as she moved toward the floor-to-ceiling windows that dominated the main living area. The afternoon sun bathed the space in natural light, offering a panoramic view of the verdant expanse and the cityscape beyond.

"The glass is electrochromic," I explained, following her to the window. "It adjusts automatically throughout the day, though you can override it manually if you prefer."

"Care for a drink?" I asked, moving toward the corner bar nestled beside a double-sided fireplace of smoked glass and blue-veined marble.

"Whiskey, neat," she replied, running her fingers along the back of the Italian leather sofa as she continued her visual exploration.

I poured us both two fingers of Talisker, the same we'd had at the castle. As I handed her the crystal tumbler, our fingers brushed.

"This penthouse is nothing like Blackmoor," she observed, accepting the drink.

"Intentionally so," I explained. "That's my heritage—this place is purely of my own design. Every system, every material, every view was my choice."

She took a sip, glancing around at the meticulous details of the space. "It's very…you."

"Would you like the complete tour?" I asked, gesturing toward the hallway that continued deeper into the residence.

"Lead the way, Lord Blackmoor," she teased.

I guided her through the main living space, pausing to point out details I was particularly proud of—the custom Italian furniture in charcoal and navy, the walnut accents that provided warmth against the coolness of marble and glass.

"The kitchen rarely sees much use when I'm here alone," I confessed as we passed through the sleek cooking space with its matte black cabinetry and brass fixtures.

"It's beautiful," Lex said, trailing her fingers along the veined quartzite countertop. "Though I suspect you didn't design all this just to order takeaway."

"You'd be surprised," I replied. "Though I do appreciate having the proper setting when I choose to cook."

We continued to the eastern wing, where the floor-to-ceiling windows offered a panoramic view of the Thames. "The master suite," I said, opening the double doors to reveal the expanse beyond.

The king-sized, platform bed faced the windows, and a sitting area with a chaise lounge created a private retreat by the window.

"The bed is positioned so you can watch the sunrise without leaving it," I explained.

"And I bet the view is equally spectacular at any hour," Lex commented with a suggestive glance.

She moved to the window, her silhouette outlined against the daylight. "You can see half of London from here."

"That's rather the point," I said, moving to stand beside her. "From this height, you can observe everything while remaining separate from it all." I motioned to another door. "The master bath is through here," I continued, leading Lex into a sanctuary-like space dominated by a freestanding soaking tub positioned by a window.

"The glass can turn opaque with a word or touch," I demonstrated, pressing a concealed panel. The window immediately frosted over, providing complete privacy.

"Though at this height, it's hardly necessary," Lex observed, walking to the center of the bathroom. "You've thought of everything, haven't you?" she asked, turning back to me.

"I try to," I said. "It's both my greatest strength and my most significant flaw, according to Tag."

We moved on to the lower level, where I showed her my private office and technical workspace. Unlike the underground ops hub at Blackmoor, this space offered stunning views while maintaining absolute privacy through the same kind of specialized glass. "Not quite as cave-like," I said, "but the equipment is comparable. The advantage here is not having to go underground to access world-class technology."

"And this is just your London office," she mused, running her fingers along the edge of one of the sleek desks.

"I've saved the best for last," I said, leading her to the sculptural, spiral staircase that wound upward.

She glanced toward the nearby lift. "Taking the scenic route?"

"The stairs offer a better reveal," I explained.

We emerged into the glass-enclosed solarium that could transform from winter garden to summer entertaining space with retractable walls. The outdoor terrace surrounded a heated infinity pool that appeared to spill into the London skyline, the afternoon sun casting golden reflections across its surface.

"Con, this is…" Lex began, then seemed to run out of words as she took in the three-hundred-and-sixty-degree view of London spread out beneath today's blue sky.

"I know," I said in a hushed tone, watching her rather than anything else.

I led her toward the far end of the rooftop, where my private helipad waited, secured by advanced authentication systems. "The helipad connects directly to the penthouse via that glass walkway."

"I suppose there are times when aerial transport is necessary," Lex commented.

We walked back toward the pool. "The water is always heated," I said. "Even in winter, you can swim while watching the infrequent snow fall over London."

Lex turned to me. "Have you ever actually done that? Swam during a snowstorm?"

I shook my head. "No. I've always meant to, but somehow, never found the right moment—or perhaps the right person to share it with."

She smiled at that, her expression softening. "It sounds magical."

"There are several other spaces I could show you," I continued, gesturing back toward the main level. "A library with a hidden bar, a media room designed for comfort, a few balconies with privacy screens."

"You've created quite the sanctuary up here," she observed. "Completely separate from the world below."

"That was the intent," I acknowledged. "A place where I could control every variable and anticipate every need."

As we made our way back to the main level, I was struck by how empty the space felt despite its perfect design. There were no personal photographs in the public areas, no mementos or keepsakes that spoke of a life beyond work and obligation.

"I just realized," I said as we returned to the main living area, "this is the first time I've given anyone the complete tour."

Lex looked at me. "Thank you for sharing it with me." She turned a slow circle, taking in the space once more.

"What do you think?" I asked, eager to hear her assessment.

"I think," she said slowly, moving closer, "that it's exactly what I would have expected from the Earl of Blackmoor—sophisticated, private, technologically superior, positioned literally above the rest of society."

I inclined my head, unsure if her evaluation was complimentary or critical.

"But," she continued, her hand finding mine, "I also think it's been waiting for someone to make it more than just a perfect space. To make it a home."

I pulled her closer. "And do you have any suggestions about who might be qualified for such a task?"

"I might," she replied, the hint of a smile playing at the corners of her mouth. "Though I'll need to conduct a more thorough inspection first. Starting with that master suite you showed me earlier."

Her fingers threaded through mine as she led me back down the hallway. The setting sun cast an amber glow, bathing her skin in warm light as we entered the bedroom. When she turned to face me, I cradled her cheeks in my hands, brushing my thumbs across her cheekbones. "I thought I'd lost you," I whispered.

"You almost did." There was no accusation in her tone, only honesty.

"I won't make that mistake again."

Her hand covered mine. "Good."

The kiss began slowly, deliberately—a different sort of apology than words could express. Her body melted against mine, the tension of our separation transforming into something electric. We moved toward the bed without breaking contact, each step a slow dance of reconciliation.

"I missed you," I whispered against her neck, though we'd been apart less than a day. The words meant so much more, and she knew it.

"Show me," she replied, and I did.

Where our previous lovemaking had been driven by urgency, this was something else—a slow, intimate exploration. When she guided me inside her, our gazes locked, the physical connection mirroring something deeper—a trust rebuilt, a partnership reforged.

We moved together in perfect rhythm, the London lights creating a backdrop of stars through the uncovered windows. As we lay entwined in the aftermath, her head on my chest, I knew with absolute certainty that this—she—was what I had been missing all along.

The digital security panel beside the bed quietly chimed to indicate that the perimeter security had automatically engaged for the night. With Lex warm and safe in my arms, I drifted into a dreamless sleep that I only experienced when with her.

I woke to the first light of dawn, Lex still asleep beside me. I watched her breathe, struck by how close I'd come to losing this before it had truly begun.

If she hadn't forgiven me, my behavior would have been the worst mistake of my life. Not being with her was unfathomable. It didn't matter that we'd known each other for only a short time; those few hours when she was gone had left me feeling like I was missing a vital piece of myself.

My secure mobile vibrated softly on the nightstand. I reached for it, not wanting to disturb her rest. The encrypted message was from Kestrel—direct and urgent.

Orlov relocated to facility near Inverness. Not Dunwich Bay, as suggested. Equipment transported via private cargo plane last night.

I frowned, reading the message twice. The certainty with which both Mr. Bennett and Dr. McLaren had identified Dunwich Bay now seemed curious. Either their intelligence was flawed, or something else was at play. My instinct leaned toward the latter.

Lex stirred beside me, her eyes opening slowly. For a moment, her expression was unguarded—soft, content—before awareness returned, and she smiled.

"You're staring," she said, her voice husky with sleep.

"I am." I brushed a strand of hair from her face. "It's a view I could get used to."

She stretched, then noticed the mobile in my hand. "Work already?"

"I'm afraid so." I showed her Kestrel's message. "What do you make of this?"

She sat up, instantly alert as she read the text. "Inverness, not Dunwich Bay." Her brow furrowed. "That's interesting, given how certain Bennett and Dr. McLaren seemed."

"My thoughts exactly."

"However, it was only one possible location," she said, her mind clearly working through the implications. "The infrastructure requirements Evelyn described could apply to several facilities along the English coast. I don't think it merits concern that they focused on one possibility."

I agreed, though something about it still nagged at me. "How do you want to handle the next steps?"

She considered the question, and I realized how different this was from our previous interaction—my deliberate choice to ask rather than direct.

"We should verify Kestrel's information independently before proceeding," she decided. "Then coordinate with MI6 and Unit 23."

"I was thinking of asking Bennett and McLaren to meet us here," I said, "but perhaps we should take the helicopter to SIS headquarters and leave for Blackmoor directly from there."

"That's more efficient," she agreed, then hesitated. "Though I'm reluctant to leave this luxurious penthouse so soon."

I smiled, brushing my lips against hers. "We can stay as long as you'd like."

She shook her head, suddenly serious. "As beautiful as this place is, I feel more comfortable at Blackmoor. It feels more like…"

"Home?" I offered when she trailed off.

"Yes," she affirmed. "Which is strange, considering I've only been there a short time."

"Not strange at all," I assured her, pulling her close once more. "Blackmoor has that effect on people who belong there."

The implication wasn't lost on either of us.

Two hours later, we touched down on VX's private helipad. Bennett and Dr. McLaren were waiting when we exited the lift on the sixth floor, both appearing unsurprised by our early arrival. We proceeded to a secure conference room where I shared Kestrel's intelligence.

"Inverness?" Bennett studied the information, his expression unreadable. "It doesn't make as much sense as Dunwich Bay; however, perhaps that's the point."

Dr. McLaren leaned forward. "I agree. It was too obvious."

"We need to be vigilant in recognizing Labyrinth's ploys of distraction," said Lex. "And at the same time, figure out exactly where they're headed."

"Roger that," Bennett said, pulling up satellite imagery of the area surrounding Inverness. "There's an old military research facility ten kilometers outside the city limits."

For the next hour, the four of us worked together, with Bennett contributing his extensive knowledge of Russian operations in Scotland. Despite my initial reservations about their earlier certainty regarding Dunwich Bay, their expertise was undeniable.

"The Inverness intel appears valid, based on what we've discovered," Bennett concluded. "I recommend we focus our efforts there."

"The question isn't just what Orlov is building," I said, "but who he's building it for. Unless Viktor is Janus, which my gut is telling me he's not, then he's merely a cog in a much larger machine."

"Agreed," Dr. McLaren said. "We should deploy immediately."

"I concur," Lex said when she realized I was awaiting her response. Never again would I proceed without it.

"We can leave within the hour," I said, pulling out my mobile to make arrangements with my pilot.

As Bennett coordinated with the MI6 team and I briefed my Unit 23 contacts, Lex and Dr. McLaren stepped aside for what appeared to be a private conversation. I couldn't hear what they were discussing, but Lex's expression was intensely focused, and her mentor's was equally serious.

"We'll travel on my plane," I announced once the briefings were complete. "There's room for the team, and it's equipped with secure communications."

As the others prepared to depart, I pulled Lex aside, our hands briefly tangling.

"Thank you," I said simply.

"For what?" she asked.

"Your forgiveness. Your willingness to work with me despite everything." I squeezed her hand gently. "I don't take it for granted."

Her smile warmed me from the inside. "I'm glad to hear it. Don't make me regret it."

"Never," I promised.

We were making our final preparations to board when my mobile vibrated with an urgent message from Tag. I frowned at the screen.

Need to speak with you immediately. Regarding Nightingale. Critical.

"Everything all right?" Lex asked, noting my expression.

"I need to make a call. I'll be just a moment."

I stepped away, dialing Tag's secure line. He answered immediately.

"She's gone," he blurted.

"What do you mean, gone?"

"Vanished," Tag's voice was tight and controlled, but I could hear the underlying tension. "Typhon doesn't even know where she is."

"When?"

"Sometime in the last twelve hours. He said that when he arrived for a check-in, the place was empty. He made contact with me to see if I'd heard from her."

I processed this information, quickly considering the implications. "I'll follow up with Kestrel," I offered. I couldn't think of any other person who might hear chatter about a missing Unit-23 operative.

"Appreciated." Tag's voice betrayed more emotion than I'd heard from him in years.

When I returned to Lex, she examined me with concern.

"Nightingale's missing," I said, keeping my tone low. As I held her gaze, I thought about Tag's voice—the raw edge conveying fear and loss—and recognized it as the exact emotion I'd felt not knowing where Lex was or if I'd get to her in time to protect her. The realization only strengthened my resolve to never let that happen again.

"I sent a message to Kestrel," I told her.

"Good thinking."

"I'm worried about him," I whispered.

"Rightly so."

"Ready?" I asked, offering her my arm.

"Ready," she confirmed, her hand sliding into the crook of my elbow.

Together, we boarded the plane that would take us north, back to Scotland, closer to answers, yet for the two of us, also closer to home and the life I hoped we'd build there when this was all over.

For Tag, though, I feared his search was just beginning. I only prayed it didn't end with the discovery that whoever put the price on Nightingale's head had found her.

16

The Georgian townhouse in Inverness, where Bennett arranged for us to stay, stood nestled among similar buildings on a quiet street. Its elegant exterior concealed a functional, modern interior—a fitting base for our operation.

"Everything's ready," Bennett said as he went through the procedures to enter the safe house. "The necessary equipment arrived and has been tested."

He led us through to what had once been a formal sitting room, now transformed into a command center with multiple monitors displaying various views of the facility outside Inverness.

Con moved immediately to examine the setup. "Impressive modifications to the standard-issue gear."

"Thank you," Bennett replied, a hint of satisfaction in his voice. "I prefer to enhance rather than replace."

I examined the satellite feed of our target—a nondescript industrial building surrounded by a high fence and minimal external features that belied its true purpose.

"The structure has three underground levels," Bennett explained, bringing up the architectural schematics. "Most activity occurs on the lowest floor, where power consumption has tripled in the past seventy-two hours."

Con and I exchanged glances. The spike aligned perfectly with what we'd expect for neural processor testing.

"Tea?" Bennett asked me. "Or perhaps something stronger after the flight?"

"Tea would be perfect, thank you," I answered.

While Bennett disappeared to the kitchen, Con leaned closer to me. "I guess what I want doesn't concern him," he said with a wink before his expression turned serious. "What's your read on him?"

"Thorough. Exacting. Possibly overcautious. But it's early."

"He's made quite the name for himself tracking Russian ops," Con agreed. "Not sure if that makes him an asset or a liability in this situation."

Bennett returned with a tray of drinks—tea for me, coffee for himself and Con, who raised a brow in my direction. We both smiled.

"Your rooms are upstairs. I've taken the liberty of arranging the corner suite for you both. Better sight lines of the street."

Bennett's acknowledgment of our relationship was subtle but clear, and I felt heat rise to my cheeks despite myself.

"The facility has unusual patterns of activity," he continued. "Night shifts have increased, and three specialized technicians arrived yesterday. My assessment is they're fully operational, which means Aberdeenshire was mostly a smokescreen."

"My assessment as well," said Con.

Dr. McLaren joined us from another room, where she'd been reviewing data. "I've analyzed the heat signatures," she said, gesturing to one of the monitors. "The patterns suggest they're running continuous tests. Likely working in shifts to maintain momentum."

Bennett turned to check another screen displaying perimeter feeds. He tapped rapidly on a tablet, adjusting camera angles and detection settings.

"We need to recalibrate these sensors," he said more to himself than to us. "The standard configuration won't detect the type of shielding Orlov typically employs."

Con raised a brow. "That's a highly specific concern."

"It's my job to anticipate these things," Bennett replied tersely. He began typing a series of commands that seemed excessive even by field operation standards. "We'll need to establish a secondary communication channel as well. And I want biometric checks for all entry points."

I caught Con's eye, noting the subtle tension in his expression that mirrored my own thoughts. Bennett's intensity was rapidly increasing.

As we broke to review our respective assignments, Dr. McLaren beckoned me to join her at a workstation in the corner of the room. Her smile was warm, maternal even, as she pulled up the schematics of the facility's electrical systems.

"I've been meaning to check in with you," she said quietly. "This mission has unique…complexities."

I understood she meant more than just the technical challenges.

"Con is quite remarkable," she continued, her eyes flickering briefly toward where he stood, deep in conversation with Bennett. "I've rarely seen anyone adapt so quickly to unfamiliar terrain."

"He's full of surprises," I agreed, unable to keep my admiration absent from my tone.

Dr. McLaren smiled knowingly. "The professional and personal lines blur easily in our work. Sometimes, that's not a bad thing." She paused, her expression growing thoughtful. "The right partner can be an anchor in stormy waters."

"I'm still figuring out the navigation," I admitted, chuckling.

"You already know what to do," she said, her hand briefly touching mine. "Your judgment has always been excellent. Both professionally and…otherwise."

"Speaking from experience?" I ventured.

Her eyes grew distant. "Once, yes. I knew what it was to find that rare connection—when two minds seem perfectly attuned." She looked down at her tablet, her voice dropping. "But sometimes, the timing fails us. He loved another and still does to this day."

I started to ask more, but she abruptly straightened, her professional demeanor snapping back into place.

"I've said too much." She looked uncomfortable. "Let's get back to these access points."

Across the room, Bennett was spreading facility blueprints across a table. As Con and I joined him, I noticed the detailed annotations Bennett had already made—patrol routes, camera blind spots, even ventilation access points, marked with a thoroughness that seemed to go beyond the information we'd received from headquarters.

"You seem to know the compound exceptionally well," I observed.

Bennett barely looked up. "I've studied similar Orlov facilities. They follow predictable patterns."

"Even down to the guard rotation schedules?" Con asked, pointing to the handwritten notes in the margins.

"Educated guesses, based on field reports," Bennett replied, but something in his tone felt defensive. "We'll verify once we're operational."

Throughout the afternoon, I noticed Bennett making brief calls from the hallway, speaking too quietly to overhear. Twice, he disappeared entirely for fifteen-minute intervals, returning with no explanation. When questioned about a camera blind spot, he provided information that hadn't been in our briefing packets.

"We should eat," Bennett announced when evening approached. "I've arranged for local catering."

The dining table had been set with surprising formality—polished silver, crystal glasses, and candles casting a warm glow over white linen. Bennett poured amber whiskey into tumblers with the solemnity of a religious ritual.

"Single malt from a distillery just north of here," he explained. "Family-owned for eleven generations."

As we ate Highland specialties—smoked salmon, venison with juniper berries, and tatties—Bennett revealed unexpected personal details. He spoke passionately about the region's history, his knowledge extending far beyond what his career would require.

"My grandmother was born in a cottage not twenty miles from here," he said, his voice softening. "She used to tell me stories about kelpies that would scare me senseless."

"You've never mentioned your Scottish heritage," Dr. McLaren remarked.

Something flashed in Bennett's eyes—a momentary sharpness quickly concealed. "There are many things we don't discuss, Evelyn."

Con steered the conversation toward lighter territory. "I was unaware of this particular safe house."

"I purchased it fifteen years ago," Bennett replied. "It was originally a standard MI6 property, but I've… personalized it over time. Few people know of its existence."

"It feels more like a home than an operational base," I observed.

Bennett smiled faintly. "Perhaps that's intentional. The best cover is often domesticity."

The conversation remained professional until Bennett, on his third glass of whiskey, began discussing Orlov with an intensity that hadn't been present earlier.

"He's methodical to the point of obsession," Bennett said, his knuckles white around his glass. "Leaves nothing to chance and trusts no one. Breaking into his operation isn't just about technology—it's about understanding how he thinks."

"You sound like you've studied him closely," I remarked.

Bennett's eyes flashed. "Our paths crossed years ago. Classified operation in Estonia. Let's just say I have personal reasons for ensuring he doesn't succeed with this neural tech."

The revelation cast a shadow over our planning. This wasn't just another assignment for Bennett—it was personal. More puzzling was Dr. McLaren's reaction. The more Malcolm spoke, the more uncomfortable she appeared, to the point of anger. Apparently, Con had picked up on it and attempted to change the subject.

"What led to your interest in joining SIS?" he asked.

My father," Bennett said, resting against his chair. "He served during the Cold War—Berlin Station, then Moscow. Some of my earliest memories are of him discussing operational security with me at the breakfast table."

"How fascinating, so you followed in his footsteps, then?" I asked, genuinely curious.

"Partly." For the first time, Bennett's expression softened slightly. "But more because I witnessed firsthand how Russian intelligence operates. The methods, the mindset, the patience. I wanted to be the counterbalance."

Con studied him with new interest. "Were you always focused solely on Russian operations?"

"For most of my career, yes." Bennett's voice took on a sharper edge. "I've tracked numerous GRU and

FSB operations across Europe. Including, at one point, Viktor Orlov's research."

His redirect back to Orlov piqued my curiosity. "Before his supposed death?"

"That's right. He was on our watch list due to his connections with military research facilities. Nothing concrete enough for action, but concerning, nonetheless."

After dinner, we returned to finalizing the preparations for tomorrow's fieldwork. As the night grew late, Bennett and Dr. McLaren eventually retired to their rooms, leaving Con and me alone in the command center.

Con moved to stand behind my chair, his hands resting lightly on my shoulders. "Interesting developments," he murmured, his breath warm against my ear.

I leaned back against him, savoring the brief moment of connection. "Bennett's reactions are becoming concerning."

"Agreed. I sense this is personal for him, and we all know how dangerous that can be."

His fingers traced a gentle pattern along my collarbone, a quiet intimacy in the midst of our professional setting. I closed my eyes briefly, allowing myself to feel the simple comfort of his touch.

"We should get some rest," I finally said, though neither of us moved immediately.

Con bent down, his lips brushing my temple. "Tomorrow will tell us more."

As we made our way upstairs to our shared room, I found myself balancing multiple complexities—the mission, Bennett's mysterious vendetta, and this deepening connection with Con that seemed to grow stronger amid the uncertainty.

The feeling of dread in the pit of my stomach become heavier, despite Con's calming presence. While AIWS was horrific on its own, I couldn't help but think that whatever was actually going on was far worse.

17

Con

I woke at zero four hundred, my mind too restless for sleep. Something about Bennett's behavior and his excessive familiarity with the Inverness facility had bothered me well into the night. Careful not to wake Lex, I slipped from the bed and made my way downstairs.

The formal sitting room—aka our command center—was dimly lit. A figure stood by the table, hunched over papers I didn't recall seeing yesterday. Bennett didn't notice me as I paused in the doorway, watching him pore over what appeared to be internal floor plans different from those he'd shared previously. What in the bloody hell was he up to? Sabotaging the mission to fulfill his vendetta?

"Found something new?" I asked.

Bennett's shoulders tensed before he turned. Nothing in his expression betrayed surprise, but the swift movement with which he gathered the papers told its own story.

"Lord Blackmoor. You're up early."

"As are you." I moved into the room, eyes on the documents he was attempting to conceal. "Those don't look like the schematics we reviewed yesterday."

"Supplementary materials," he replied smoothly. "MI6 sent additional intelligence overnight."

"At two in the morning?"

"Russian operations don't adhere to business hours." He folded the papers and tucked them under his tablet. "Coffee?"

"Please."

While he busied himself in the kitchen, I glanced at the edge of a document that was still visible from where he'd stashed it. Annotations marked what appeared to be security rotation schedules—far more specific than any information we'd discussed.

"Your intelligence is remarkably thorough," I commented as he handed me a mug.

"As I said yesterday, Russian operations are my specialty."

"So specific, though. Guard rotations, maintenance schedules…" I sipped the coffee. "Almost as if you've been inside the facility."

His eyes narrowed almost imperceptibly. "Good intelligence often provides that level of detail."

"Of course."

Bennett gathered his materials. "I need to make some calls before we finalize today's approach. The equipment I requested will arrive by zero seven hundred."

After he left, I extracted my mobile and messaged Gus. *Need Malcolm Bennett background ASAP. Focus on any Orlov connection.*

His reply came a few minutes later. *On it. Something interesting in Estonia records. Will update soon.*

When I returned upstairs, Lex was awake, hair tousled from sleep. My body responded immediately to the sight of her, desire momentarily overriding my concern.

"You're up early." She stretched her arms above her head, revealing a naked breast. I raised a brow, and she covered herself.

"Bennett's downstairs with floor plans I've never seen before."

Her expression sharpened. "MI6 wouldn't withhold that level of intelligence from a joint operation."

"My thoughts exactly." I sat beside her on the bed. "I've asked Gus to dig deeper."

"Good." She snuggled against me, further testing my resolve to focus on work rather than her naked body pressed against mine. "What did these new documents show?" she asked as her hand snaked around my waist.

"Internal security protocols, maintenance schedules, and what looked like staff rotations." I covered her hand, stopping her from venturing any lower. "The level of detail suggests firsthand knowledge."

"That's concerning," she agreed. "Especially given his fixation on Orlov."

"We'll need to watch him closely today."

"Do we?" she murmured, wriggling from my grasp, her palm landing on my hardening cock.

"I suppose Bennett and the demise of civilization can wait a bit longer," I said, standing to pull my shirt over my head and drop my trousers.

By zero eight hundred, Tag arrived with two Unit-23 operatives. His expression as he greeted me spoke volumes—whatever brought him here wasn't routine support.

"Typhon sent us," he explained once we were alone. "Said you might need additional resources."

"Perfect timing," I replied, then led him into the command center, where I made introductions to the others in the room. "Malcolm Bennett, MI6."

Tag shook his hand. "Your reputation precedes you."

"As does yours, Mr. MacTaggert," Bennett replied coolly.

Tag raised a brow, then turned to me. "This is Callen Cavendish, code name Renegade, and Kiernan Lockhart, code name Archon."

After shaking their hands, I looked around for Lex, but when I found her head-to-head with Dr. McLaren, I suggested they get settled and I'd make the rest of the introductions later.

While the two men finalized the equipment checks, Tag pulled me aside. "I received a message that was supposedly from Nightingale. Said to trust no one who 'claims to know the labyrinth from within.'"

"Supposedly?"

"Still trying to confirm."

"Interesting." I glanced toward Bennett, who was now unfolding yet another set of diagrams I hadn't seen. "Our MI6 colleague seems to have an unusual depth of knowledge about this facility."

"So I noticed." Tag's eyes narrowed.

When we rejoined the group, Bennett was displaying interior layouts showing ventilation systems, power junctions, even what appeared to be staff rotation schedules.

"These are remarkably detailed," I observed. "Recent acquisition?"

"I have my sources," Bennett replied, the evasion obvious.

Throughout the rest of the morning, I monitored the intelligence feeds while keeping Bennett in my peripheral vision. His movements carried the confidence of someone on familiar ground rather than an analyst working from reports.

"We've intercepted communications about a demonstration scheduled to take place in two days," I announced after decoding a series of messages. "Zero nine hundred hours. References to 'observer protocols' and 'final integration parameters.'"

Bennett's reaction was immediate—a flash of what looked like panic before he quickly steeled it. "My God, we aren't yet prepared to intercept," he stated, fingers tightening on the edge of the table.

"We will be," I said, glancing over at Tag and Lex, who both discreetly nodded.

"We're all aware of the stakes, Infidel," Dr. McLaren interjected, her tone measured. "However, hasty action could jeopardize everything."

Bennett turned to her, something unspoken passing between them. "You of all people should understand the urgency, Evelyn."

The use of her first name hung in the air, laden with history neither had disclosed.

"I understand perfectly, Malcolm," she replied quietly. "Which is why we must be methodical."

Throughout the afternoon, we tracked the activity at the facility while Bennett grew increasingly agitated about the impending test. His personal stake became more apparent with each passing hour.

"We need to identify all emergency exits," he declared, marking points on the facility diagram that weren't indicated in our official briefings. "Orlov will have contingencies for rapid evacuation."

"You seem rather certain of his methods," Tag observed casually.

Bennett's eyes flashed. "I've studied his operational patterns for years. He maintains consistent security protocols."

"Most scientists don't have security protocols," I noted.

"Orlov isn't most scientists." Bennett turned to Dr. McLaren. "Tell them, Evelyn."

She hesitated a few seconds, then spoke. "Viktor always maintained unusual awareness of defensive measures. Even at conferences, he insisted on specific security arrangements."

"That's professional caution," I countered. "Bennett's describing intimate knowledge of personal habits."

The tension in the room thickened as Bennett produced yet another set of detailed plans—this time showing what appeared to be the living quarters inside the facility, complete with notations about the surveillance blind spots.

"These aren't in any MI6 file," Lex stated flatly.

"My sources are more comprehensive than the official channels," Bennett replied, a defensive edge creeping into his voice.

"This is unacceptable," said Lex, raising her chin. "You were the one who insisted we follow strict protocols, yet now you're the one operating outside of your own ground rules."

Tag caught my eye across the table, the subtle arch of his eyebrow communicating our shared suspicion.

Bennett shifted on his feet but didn't speak.

"Malcolm, name your sources, or I'll call for your immediate removal from the mission," Lex persisted.

"You can't do that."

"Watch me." She pulled out her mobile, but before she could place a call, Bennett relented.

"I'll send you the list."

"Not only to me, to the entire team."

"But—"

Lex shook her head. "It's what you demanded from Con and Unit 23. Either MI6 does the same or, again, you'll be dismissed."

He sputtered some more, mumbling unintelligibly.

"Well done," I said, pulling Lex close to me and nuzzling her neck.

Rather than walk away, she kissed my cheek and leaned in closer. "I'll admit that felt bloody good. I've grown tired of his prevarication."

While it was on the tip of my tongue to suggest that Dr. McLaren was guilty of the same, at least in my opinion, I kept those thoughts to myself.

As evening approached, Dr. McLaren suggested a tactical approach that aligned with my own assessment—immediate observation rather than intervention, and gathering evidence before determining our response. Bennett argued for more aggressive measures but was outvoted.

"You're making a mistake," he said, but ultimately conceded.

Throughout dinner, which Tag's team prepared, Bennett remained withdrawn, checking his mobile with increasing frequency.

After the meal, we broke into teams to prepare the equipment for tomorrow's surveillance. Dr. McLaren joined me to calibrate the long-range monitoring devices.

"Bennett's investment in this mission seems personal," I commented quietly.

She hesitated before responding. "Malcolm's history with Russian operations—I'll just say that some wounds never fully heal."

"What kind of history?"

"That's for him to share, if he chooses." Her tone indicated the subject was closed, but I filed away her reaction for further consideration.

As darkness fell, we established our final protocols for tomorrow's op. Bennett remained professional despite his earlier outburst, contributing intel about the facility's perimeter defenses that proved accurate when cross-referenced with the satellite imagery.

When we concluded our planning, Tag and his team took the first watch while the rest of us prepared to get what sleep we could before tomorrow's critical operation.

Lex and I retreated to our room.

"What a day," she said once we were alone.

"I'm increasingly concerned about Bennett's mental state."

Her eyes opened wide. "Mental state?"

"His reactions are inappropriate."

"You're right, I suppose."

"There's something else." I reiterated what Dr. McLaren said about some wounds never healing and that, when I pressed for more details, she said it was up to him whether or not to share.

"I don't like that one bit." Lex shook her head. "I'll see what I can find out from Evelyn tomorrow."

While we held each other close, we didn't make love. We were both exhausted as much as overwhelmed by what the days ahead would bring. Once I was certain Lex was asleep, I leaned forward and whispered, "I love you." She hadn't said those words to me yet, and while that stung a bit, I knew she cared, and that was enough for now.

18

Lex

The clock on the bedside table read zero four hundred when my eyes opened. Con's side of the bed was empty, though I hadn't heard him leave. My mind immediately began cataloging the mounting complications—Bennett's increasingly suspicious behavior, the impending demonstration of what could be the most dangerous weapons system in history, and my conflicted feelings about the man whose scent still lingered on the sheets beside me. Con had become my ally, my lover, and potentially my greatest distraction at a time when focus was essential.

After showering and dressing, I made my way down the corridor, toward the stairs. Halfway there, I paused at the sound of a hushed voice coming from one of the rooms. The door stood slightly ajar, and through the gap, I saw Bennett pacing, mobile pressed to his ear.

"Chan eil e ullamh fhathast," he seethed. *"Feumaidh sinn barrachd ùine."*

While I couldn't understand all the words, his tone conveyed urgency. He glanced toward the door, and I retreated quickly, continuing down the hallway as if I'd just emerged from my room.

The timing of Bennett's secretive call—before anyone else was supposed to be awake—combined with his earlier behavior, heightened my unease.

I went downstairs, walking softly out of habit rather than necessity. When I reached the bottom, I heard Con's voice from the sitting room—now our command center. He was speaking with Tag.

"The documents he produced last night contained details not even Unit 23 has access to," Con said. "How would MI6 obtain that level of information without field observation?"

"They wouldn't," Tag replied. "Unless—"

I rounded the corner, and both men fell silent, looking up at me. Con's expression softened immediately, his eyes warming.

"Morning," he greeted, offering me a cup of tea from the tray beside him. "Sleep well?"

"As well as can be expected," I replied. "Anything new?"

"Surveillance equipment is in place," Tag responded. "Renegade and Archon installed perimeter monitoring overnight. We have eyes on all external access points."

Con studied my face. "Something wrong?"

I debated sharing what I'd overheard, but decided to wait until we were alone. "Just thinking through everything from yesterday," I said. "Where's Dr. McLaren?"

"Already reviewing the data feeds," Tag replied. "She's been up for hours. Maybe never went to bed."

An hour later, we gathered in the command center for a final briefing. Bennett appeared composed, no trace of his earlier agitation visible as he outlined our objectives for the day. His hands moved with confidence across the maps, highlighting the observation points and potential vulnerabilities.

"Initial monitoring only," he emphasized, his gaze sweeping over all of us. "No contact or intervention without explicit authorization. If Orlov is there, I want visual confirmation, but absolutely no engagement."

The authority in his voice made me wonder again about his history with the Russian scientist. The personal vendetta Bennett harbored seemed to run deep.

We broke into teams—Con and I would observe from a mobile position at the western approach, while

Bennett and Tag would watch the facility's main entrance. Dr. McLaren would coordinate from the safe house, with Renegade and Archon handling the perimeter security.

As we prepared our equipment, I found myself alone with Con in the gear room.

"I need to tell you something," I said, lowering my voice. "Bennett was on a call this morning—speaking Gaelic. I couldn't hear him well enough to understand what he was saying, but he was agitated, looking over his shoulder like he was afraid of discovery."

Con's brow furrowed. "That aligns with what Gus just sent me. Bennett has connections to this region that go beyond what he's disclosed to MI6." He checked that the door was closed before continuing. "His obsession with Orlov appears individualized—their paths crossed in Estonia during a mission that ended in disaster."

"What kind of disaster?"

"Unclear. Records are heavily redacted, but whatever happened, it left lasting scars." Con's gaze locked with mine. "I suspect that's what's driving him now."

I tucked the information away, wondering why Viper hadn't briefed me on it. More, why Bennett was still an active agent. "We need to watch him closely."

"Already on it." Con brushed a strand of hair from my face, the brief touch lingering. "Be careful today."

"I always am," I replied, the corners of my mouth lifting.

"That's debatable, given how you stormed into my castle and hacked my systems," he said with a half smile.

"That wasn't recklessness," I countered. "That was a calculated risk."

His smile widened. "And was I worth the risk, Dr. Sterling?"

The lightness in his tone did nothing to diminish the weight of the question. "The jury's still deliberating," I said, but couldn't keep my own smile from emerging.

Dr. McLaren entered before Con could respond. "Vehicle is ready for your departure," she announced, her sharp eyes moving between us. "The eastern approach has been cleared. Tag and Bennett are already in position."

En route to our observation point, Con drove while I prepared our equipment. The day was clear but cold, the Scottish landscape breathtaking even as we focused on what was ahead. We parked the unmarked vehicle in a wooded area with clear sight lines to the western side of the facility, then set up our monitoring station.

"Range check," I said into my comms.

"Clear," came Dr. McLaren's voice. "All channels operational."

The facility looked unassuming from our vantage point—a series of industrial buildings surrounded by perimeter fencing with security checkpoints at each entrance. Nothing in its external appearance hinted at the neural weapons development we believed was occurring inside.

"Movement at the south gate," Con observed, adjusting his binoculars. "Delivery vehicle approaching."

I documented the arrival, noting the corporate markings on the side—another shell company, no doubt, providing components for Labyrinth.

Our surveillance revealed steady activity at the facility—deliveries, security patrols, staff rotations. Nothing beyond what we'd anticipated until midmorning, when I intercepted a transmission on one of the frequencies we were monitoring.

"I've got something," I whispered, adjusting the parameters. The communication was encoded but with known Russian military protocols. I applied a decryption algorithm, and fragments of text appeared on my screen.

—Sterling's expertise critical for neural interface refinement—

—acquisition rather than elimination—

—within 48 hours—

—ensure complete neural mapping before integration—

"They're talking about you," Con said, leaning closer to read the fragments. His shoulder pressed against mine. "They want you alive."

I shivered despite the warmth in the vehicle. "For the neural interface."

"The component Kestrel mentioned was failing." Con's expression hardened. "They think you can solve their problems."

"These fragments of text mentioning me specifically have to come from high up. From Janus directly, perhaps," I said.

While he didn't speak, Con's expression darkened.

I swallowed, trying to focus on the implications rather than the personal threat. "If they're having integration issues, it means they're even further along than we thought. Neural mapping suggests direct human-machine interface capability."

"Which aligns with what we know about Orlov's previous research," Con agreed. "The question is how far they've progressed with autonomous decision-making."

I relayed our findings to Dr. McLaren through secure channels, transcribing the intercepted fragments verbatim.

"Hold position," came her response after a brief pause. "Continue monitoring but maintain cover at all costs. I'm running analysis on the transmission pattern."

An hour later, Dr. McLaren contacted us directly, her voice tight with concern.

"I've identified unusual electromagnetic signatures around the facility perimeter," she said. "They've implemented a detection grid that wouldn't appear on standard scans. Your current monitoring approach would have triggered their systems within the next hour without adjustment."

She transmitted the modified parameters that, when implemented, rendered our surveillance invisible to the facility's defenses. Her expertise proved invaluable—we would have been compromised without her intervention.

"How did you spot that?" I asked, genuinely impressed.

"I developed countermeasures for similar systems at SIS," she replied. "Orlov's signature is distinctive—he layers defensive measures in patterns most people wouldn't think to check for."

Con looked at me, eyebrow raised. I nodded, acknowledging that Dr. McLaren had once again proven herself an essential ally.

As afternoon approached, I focused on the facility's power systems, mapping the energy fluctuations through thermal imaging and electromagnetic detection.

"Look at this," I said, highlighting anomalies in the data. "The electromagnetic shielding extends far beyond the standard requirements for AI research." I indicated specific readings on the display. "And these power storage units..." I pointed to spikes in the information. "They're designed for massive energy accumulation and release, not just AI processing."

Con studied the screen, eyes narrowing. "What in the bloody hell are they building in there?"

I cross-referenced the patterns with known weapons systems in my mental catalog. "This configuration suggests integration with broadcast technology." I pulled up a schematic, sketching potential layouts. "They're not just processing information—they're preparing to transmit something. The component arrangement indicates a signal amplification and directional propagation."

"An amplified signal?"

"Capable of affecting electronics across considerable distance," I confirmed, running the calculations. "Jesus. This is bad, Con."

"Strategic deployment. Global implications," he replied.

"Precisely." I felt a cold dread settling in my stomach. "If they've solved the neural interface issue, they could potentially link human control to a system capable of affecting the electronic infrastructure worldwide."

We documented our findings and transmitted the data back to Dr. McLaren for analysis. As the daylight began to fade, movement near the facility's main entrance caught our attention.

A gaunt figure emerged, flanked by security personnel—Viktor Orlov. Through our high-powered lens, I observed him consulting with the technicians beside a delivery vehicle. His hands gestured as though he was explaining complex concepts, pointing to specific components being unloaded.

"Tag, Bennett—do you have visual?" Con asked through the comms.

"Affirmative," Tag replied.

Bennett's voice came through next, tightly controlled yet vibrating with emotion. "That's him. The bastard hasn't changed."

Despite the hatred in Bennett's words, I detected something else—a grudging professional respect in his tone as he continued, "His work was revolutionary. If only he'd applied it ethically."

"What exactly is he examining?" I asked, adjusting our camera for better resolution.

"Specialized hardware for the interface system," Bennett replied.

I captured several images as Orlov inspected what appeared to be a cylindrical device with intricate wiring.

"He's always been hands-on," Bennett commented. "Never trusted anyone else with the final inspection."

The personal knowledge in that statement reinforced my suspicions about Bennett's undisclosed history with Orlov. What exactly had happened between them?

After Orlov returned inside, we intercepted additional communications about testing schedules. References to "neural interface calibration" and "integration parameters" confirmed our suspicions about the system's development phase.

"These power configurations," I explained to Con, analyzing the data flowing across our monitors. "They're designed for broad-area effect rather than focused application. Whatever they're testing has the capacity to influence electronics across regions, not just isolated targets."

"Weaponized signal propagation," Con deduced, his mind following the same path mine had. "A broadcast that could potentially disable defense systems and communications networks."

"If merged with AIWS technology, it could theoretically affect human cognition directly."

Con's eyes met mine, understanding dawning. "Mass influence."

"It's still theoretical," I cautioned. "But the components they're assembling suggest they're moving beyond theory toward practical application."

As the sun finally set, we observed a shift change among the security personnel.

"These aren't typical guards," Con noted. "More likely, former special forces."

"Russian, by the looks of it. Bratva provides muscle for state-sponsored operations when deniability is required."

Our surveillance continued as darkness fell fully, with rotating teams maintaining observation. When Tag relieved us at zero two hundred, Con and I returned to the safe house to process our findings.

Dr. McLaren met us in the command center, her expression grave as she reviewed our data. Bennett sat nearby, studying facility schematics with intense focus.

"The neural interface applications are beyond anything I anticipated," Dr. McLaren admitted, scrolling through our readings. "This moves beyond targeted weapons systems toward something far more insidious."

"Mass disruption capability," Bennett agreed, not looking up from his maps. "But they can't have solved the autonomous integration issue yet. The human operator would still be required for precise targeting."

"Unless they've developed a true AI decision matrix," I countered. "Orlov's previous research suggested he was close to a breakthrough on self-learning neural networks."

"Without ethical constraints," Con added grimly.

While Dr. McLaren and Con discussed tactical responses, I noticed minor discrepancies in our surveillance logs—timestamps that didn't align, access records showing data retrieval from locations we hadn't authorized. Small signs that pointed to an information leakage.

I quietly began tracing the data access patterns, careful to mask my own investigation. Cross-referencing user activities, I found clues that pointed toward Bennett. His access signatures appeared in areas beyond his assigned parameters, always during brief periods when he'd stepped away from the team.

The evidence wasn't conclusive but raised serious questions. Why would Bennett access files without telling us? Where was that information going? I kept my discovery to myself temporarily, needing more evidence before making accusations. The thought of confronting him filled me with unease—not fear, but the dread of an internal betrayal when we faced such overwhelming external threats.

"You should rest," Con said, touching my shoulder. "We have eastern approach surveillance in three hours."

"Wake me if anything changes," I said, accepting how exhausted I felt.

In our room, Con pulled me close as soon as the door closed. "You've been quiet," he murmured against my hair.

"I found something concerning in the data logs, but I need more information before sharing it widely," I replied, allowing myself to lean into his strength.

He pulled back, looking into my eyes. "Bennett?"

"Yes," I responded, not questioning how he'd known. Our minds seemed increasingly synchronized, each anticipating the other's thoughts.

"My gut is telling me he can't be trusted," he admitted. "Gus is running background checks that go deeper than the standard MI6 clearance."

"Do you think he's working with the consortium?"

Con considered this. "Not directly. His hatred for Orlov seems genuine. But he's withholding information for reasons of his own."

"We need to watch him closely," I said, echoing my earlier sentiment.

"Already on it," Con replied, his lips brushing mine in a gentle kiss that deepened as I responded.

For a brief moment, the mission receded, leaving only us—two people finding connection amid the chaos. His hands framed my face as he drew back, his eyes serious.

"When this is over," he began.

"Let's focus on getting through it first," I interrupted, not ready to contemplate a future that felt increasingly uncertain.

"Sleep. I'll wake you when it's time," he said, appearing to understand without taking offense.

Three hours later, we were back on surveillance rotation. This time, Con and I took the eastern approach, concealed in dense woodland with visibility of the facility's secondary entrance.

The morning air hung heavy with mist as we settled into our observation point. Despite the minimal sleep,

I felt alert, the adrenaline sharpening my senses. Con's presence beside me provided a strange comfort despite the looming danger.

In the quiet moments between monitoring activities, I found myself studying his profile—the man was the most handsome I'd ever seen. And to think—he loved me. I looked back on how my life had changed since storming into his castle and challenging his systems. How what began as a professional rivalry had transformed into something I'd never expected to find.

"What?" he asked, catching me watching him.

"Nothing." I turned back to my equipment, but he reached out, his fingers brushing mine.

"Tell me."

I hesitated, my emotions threatening to overwhelm me. "I was thinking how different this would be without you here."

His eyes softened. "Better or worse?"

"Both." I attempted a smile. "Better because you're brilliant and I trust your judgment. Worse because now I have something to lose."

The words escaped before I could reconsider them. Con's expression shifted, understanding dawning in his eyes.

"Lex—"

"We should focus," I interrupted, not ready to pursue that conversation with so much at stake. "The mission comes first."

We returned to our surveillance, but the moment had shifted something between us. I knew then, with absolute clarity, that I had fallen in love with Conrad Carnegie. The realization terrified me, not for what it meant about us, but for how it complicated everything in this increasingly dangerous operation.

Love created vulnerability. Vulnerability led to mistakes. And mistakes in our line of work cost lives. Yet despite this rational assessment, I couldn't regret what was between us. If anything, it strengthened my resolve to see this mission through, to ensure we both had a future beyond Labyrinth.

By midmorning, our monitoring devices captured unusual activity at the facility's eastern entrance.

Equipment was being moved while technicians gathered around what appeared to be testing apparatus.

"They're preparing for something," I whispered, adjusting our visual feed for better clarity.

"Demonstration rehearsal?" Con suggested, referring to the event scheduled for the following day.

"Possibly." I enhanced the image, focusing on the equipment being assembled. "That looks like signal-transmission gear."

A side door opened, and Orlov emerged accompanied by security personnel.

I adjusted our camera for better visibility, zooming in on the testing area. Through the lens, I could see Orlov's face clearly as he supervised the preparations. His features were thinner than I remembered, but his eyes retained the same intense focus.

Then, unexpectedly, he paused.

His head turned slowly, gaze tracking across the tree line until it seemed to settle directly on our hidden position. A chill ran through me as his thin lips curved into what could only be described as a knowing smile.

"He sees us." I gasped.

Con tensed beside me. "Impossible. We're completely concealed."

Yet Orlov continued staring in our direction, his smile widening before he deliberately turned away, resuming his work as if nothing had happened.

"He knows we're watching," I said, absolute certainty in my voice. "And worse—he's been expecting us all along."

19

Con

"Get down," I hissed, pulling Lex away from the observation point and deeper into the cover of the trees. My hand gripped her arm as we retreated, staying low to avoid detection.

"He saw us," Lex whispered once we were safely concealed. Her eyes held no fear, only sharp calculation as she processed what we'd witnessed.

"That wasn't a coincidence," I replied, checking our surveillance equipment to ensure it wasn't compromised. "Orlov deliberately sought out our location."

Lex tilted her head in agreement, her expression grim. "But how? We were hidden, equipment masked against detection."

"We need to pull back. Now." I quickly gathered our gear. "If Orlov knows we're watching, this entire op could be at risk."

We made our way through the dense woodland to our vehicle, maintaining radio silence until we were clear of the facility's perimeter. Only when we were moving did I contact the others.

"Tag, we may be compromised. Orlov made direct visual contact with our position. Returning to base."

"Copy that," came Tag's terse reply. "Bennett and I will hold position until further notice."

Lex frowned beside me. "He should withdraw too. If Orlov spotted us—"

"Bennett won't leave," I interrupted. "He's been hunting Viktor for years. Now that we've confirmed his location, Bennett would sooner die than abandon his position."

The drive back to the safe house took twenty minutes, each passing kilometer deepening my concern. Not just about Orlov's awareness of our presence, but about Bennett's increasingly suspicious behavior—his excessive knowledge of the facility's layouts, his secretive calls, and his barely contained emotional reactions when Orlov's name was mentioned.

Dr. McLaren met us at the door, her expression betraying concern. "What happened?"

"Orlov knew we were there," Lex explained as we moved into the command center. "He looked directly at our position and smiled."

"That's not possible," Dr. McLaren said, but her tone lacked conviction.

My secure mobile vibrated with an incoming message—Gus's full report on Bennett. I scanned it while Lex updated Dr. McLaren on what we'd observed.

What I read confirmed my worst suspicions. Malcolm Bennett's background contained disturbing inconsistencies. His record indicated he'd started with MI6 in 1996, yet there were periods where his assignments were suspiciously thin on details.

The Estonia operation that had been redacted in earlier reports was now partially visible. Bennett had been part of a joint task force monitoring Soviet-era facilities for potential technology transfer. During that op, something had gone catastrophically wrong, resulting in the deaths of three agents.

The report named Viktor Orlov as a person of interest in that incident, not as a perpetrator, but as a potential asset who had either been turned or compromised.

Bennett was the only survivor of the team assigned to make contact with him.

Most concerning was a notation from a psychological evaluation conducted six months after Estonia. "Subject displays signs of unresolved trauma and fixation on target. Recommend continued monitoring and possible reassignment."

I slipped away to contact Tag, finding a quiet corner of the house where our conversation wouldn't be overheard.

"I've got Gus's report," I said when he answered. "Bennett's history with Orlov goes deeper than we suspected."

"I figured as much," Tag replied. "He maintains a well-crafted facade, but his control slips whenever Orlov is mentioned. His body language shifts, his pupils dilate, and his voice changes pitch."

"Watch him closely," I cautioned. "And, Tag—don't share anything sensitive with him until I return. I have concerns about where our information is going."

"Copy that." Tag paused. "Bennett received a call about fifteen minutes ago. Stepped away to take it. Returned looking resolved, somehow."

Once he rang off, I went to find Lex, who was reviewing our surveillance footage in the command center.

"I need to speak with you," I said, gesturing toward the garden door. She followed without question, both of us knowing the walls might have ears.

Outside, the cold Scottish air bit through my jacket as we walked along the perimeter of the property, staying within sight of the house, but beyond hearing distance.

"Gus sent Bennett's full background," I began. "As I said previously, he was involved in an op in Estonia that went wrong."

"What happened?"

"Three agents dead. Bennett, the sole survivor." I outlined what I'd learned, watching her expression shift from concern to grim understanding.

Her head cocked. "I can't help but wonder why Viper didn't brief me on what happened in Estonia."

"Or why Typhon didn't do the same."

We circled back toward the house, strategizing our next move. As we approached, Renegade appeared at the back door.

"Sir, we've finished analyzing the data from the eastern surveillance. You'll want to see this."

Inside, the command center had transformed into a hub of activity. Archon was enhancing thermal imagery while Dr. McLaren studied the electromagnetic readings from our morning surveillance.

"These readings reveal something worse," Lex said, moving to the main display. "What we captured goes beyond neural processing." Her fingers traced over the readout. "These wave formations match the directed energy technology research from twenty years ago."

I studied the data, connections forming as I remembered the classified information from decades past. "This matches theoretical designs for pulse weapons," I said. "Projects shelved due to targeting flaws and ethical objections."

"Not shelved," Lex corrected. "Just hidden from view."

"Good God," I hissed. "They're developing something far beyond autonomous AI," I said, my voice dropping. "A system capable of crippling global electronic networks."

"An AIWS-guided pulse weapon," Lex confirmed. "Targeted enough for strikes against specific systems or powerful enough for regional blackouts."

"If they've solved the neural-interface issue—" Dr. McLaren began.

"They could deploy it with extraordinary control," I finished. "Selecting targets based on real-time adaptive algorithms rather than pre-programmed coordinates."

Bennett entered the room as we were discussing this theory. His reaction wasn't the shock or alarm I'd expected. Instead, his expression showed resignation, as if our discovery was inevitable.

"You've figured it out," he said, moving to the display. "It's worse than you think. The integration capabilities would allow for selective targeting, including taking out defense systems while leaving civilian infrastructure intact, or vice versa."

"You knew," I accused, keeping my tone measured despite the anger rising inside me. "You knew what they were constructing and didn't share that information."

Bennett's eyes hardened. "I've been tracking Orlov's work for years. His research into neural interfaces was always headed in this direction."

"Why withhold critical intelligence from your own team?" Lex demanded.

"Because I wasn't certain," Bennett replied, though the lie was evident in his tense posture. "And because

MI6 has a history of bureaucratic hesitation when faced with unprecedented threats."

Dr. McLaren stepped forward. "Malcolm's concerns aren't unfounded," she said. "The technical specs suggest capabilities beyond anything we've encountered. A system that could selectively disable communication networks, power grids, defense installations—all with the adaptability of artificial intelligence guiding its deployment."

Her detailed knowledge raised fresh questions in my mind. How did she know so much about a system that had supposedly never been built?

"We need to abort this mission and call for military intervention," Bennett declared. "This is beyond our operational scope."

"A military strike would be too blunt an instrument," I countered. "We need a targeted approach in which we identify the key components, extract the essential personnel, and neutralize the threat without collateral damage."

"Agreed," Lex said. "A military approach risks pushing them to accelerate their timeline. Or worse, deploy what they've already built."

The debate continued, but I remained steadfast in my previously stated opinion. Throughout the discussion, I couldn't shake the feeling that Bennett was playing a role, his arguments designed to delay rather than advance our mission.

Tag walked in just as we were finishing our assessment. He pulled me aside after being briefed on our discoveries.

"I might have a lead on Nightingale," he said, keeping his voice low. "Nothing concrete yet, but signals analysis picked up communication patterns consistent with her methods. It's being tracked."

"Good," I replied. "Keep me posted."

As the team prepared for the next observation rotation, I developed a strategy to identify if there was a leak. I created three separate mission briefs with minor variations in locations and timing, ensuring each version had unique details that could be traced.

"I'll have Gus drop these by Blackmoor's courier system," I told Tag. "Each person gets a different iteration. If there is a breach, we'll know the source."

"Smart," he agreed. "Though risky if we're working against the clock."

"A calculated risk," I countered. "Better than moving forward with a compromised operational security."

The day wore on, each hour bringing new data from our field teams and increasing tension within the safe house.

By sixteen hundred hours, I was mentally exhausted, but no less vigilant. When Lex suggested we take a break to review our findings in private, I readily agreed, needing a moment away from the charged atmosphere of the command center.

We retreated to the bedroom we shared, which I'd already swept for listening devices. The wood-paneled room offered a temporary sanctuary from the chaos below.

"What happens if they succeed?" I asked Lex as we sat on the bed, in each other's arms. "If Orlov deploys this system—even as a demonstration—the implications for global stability would be catastrophic."

"It would redefine warfare," she replied, her voice soft but firm. "Nations with this technology could hold entire countries hostage without firing a single conventional weapon. Financial systems, medical equipment, and transportation networks—all vulnerable to selective attacks."

"The end of civilization as we know it," I said, staring into the distance. "Not with nuclear fire, but with silent, invisible pulses rendering our technology useless."

Lex snuggled closer. "We won't let that happen."

In her reassuring presence, I found a balance I'd never known before—someone who understood both sides of my life and who matched my intellect and determination with her own.

"Lex," I began, turning to face her. "Whatever happens in the next forty-eight hours—"

"Don't," she interrupted, her eyes meeting mine. "I need to tell you something first. I've been trying to find the right moment, but there isn't one, not in the middle of all this." She took a breath. "Con, I—"

A sharp knock at the door cut her off. Archon stood in the doorway, tablet in hand. "Satellite imagery just came in," he said. "You need to see this immediately."

We followed him downstairs, where the team had gathered around the display. The images showed a small clearing about a kilometer from the main facility.

In the center stood what appeared to be testing apparatus surrounded by multiple vehicles.

"These were taken fifteen minutes ago," Tag explained, advancing the sequence. "Watch what happens."

The next images showed a pulse of energy emanating from the central device, followed by the immediate shutdown of all electronics in a measured radius around the site.

"They're testing it," Lex said, her face pale. "A small-scale demonstration of targeted EMP capability."

"The real demonstration is tomorrow," Bennett said, his voice hollow. "This was just the rehearsal."

My eyes met Lex's, both of us understanding the gravity of what we'd witnessed. Orlov wasn't just building a weapon; he was preparing to unveil it to whoever had funded his research. And we had less than twenty-four hours to stop him.

20

Lex

The pieces of Project Labyrinth were beginning to fall into place. Based on the intel we'd gathered, Orlov's operation appeared to combine AIWS with electromagnetic pulse technology in ways we hadn't previously encountered. Our next step was clear—we needed to infiltrate the lab to confirm our suspicions and gather concrete evidence.

I observed Con from across the command center as he finalized three separate mission briefs. Each contained slight variations in coordinates and timing—a subtle trap designed to expose any leak.

When he finished, he gave me a slight nod. "We're ready."

Bennett entered the room, his posture rigid with tension. The strained dynamic between him and Con had become impossible to ignore, with team members exchanging uneasy glances whenever they occupied the same space.

"Are those our mission specs?" Bennett asked.

"Affirmative," said Con. "Infiltration scheduled for zero one hundred hours."

Dr. McLaren settled beside me as I checked my equipment. "Your access module will need to interface with their quantum-encrypted systems," she said, her voice low. "The Metzger H-series firewalls they're using have a vulnerability in the authentication handshake—exploit that, and you'll have administrative access."

I paused, my hands hovering over my gear. "How do you know they're using Metzger H-series?"

Her smile didn't reach her eyes. "It was in the intelligence briefing."

Except it wasn't. I'd memorized every line of it. There had been no mention of specific firewall systems.

Across the room, Bennett was loading his weapons. I caught a glimpse of what looked like unusual ammunition being tucked into his vest pocket—cartridges with what appeared to be red casings, though I couldn't be certain from my position. If they were what I suspected—specialized armor-piercing rounds—they weren't standard-issue or on our approved equipment list.

When he thought no one was watching, he stepped into the hallway and spoke in hushed tones. The language wasn't English—it sounded harsh, with guttural consonants. I couldn't place it, but something about the secretive nature of his actions raised more flags in my mind.

I needed to tell Con about what I'd discovered. I approached him as he secured the operations center.

"Con, I need to—"

A comms alert interrupted us. Con checked the secure line, his expression darkening. "Surveillance just picked up increased activity at the compound. We need to accelerate our timeline."

"But there's something you should know—"

"We'll have to debrief later," he said, his attention already shifting to the tactical displays. "If we miss this window, we may not get another."

I swallowed my frustration. The mission had to take priority, but the warning in my gut grew stronger with each passing hour.

We approached the facility at the designated time under a moonless sky that rendered the countryside in shades of black and gray. According to the satellite imagery, the complex sprawled across three hectares was surrounded by an electric fence and patrolled by armed guards.

"This is where we split up," Con whispered. "Each of you, follow your targeted infiltration points. Radio silence unless absolutely necessary."

While McLaren and Archon were assigned to the western perimeter, Bennett and Renegade were heading east, toward the equipment-testing field we'd observed in the satellite footage. Con and I headed for the main building, where we hoped to find data on Project Labyrinth's functionality and scope.

We'd barely cleared the perimeter when alarms shattered the night. Not at our position—they'd triggered on the opposite side.

"Why in the bloody hell is McLaren over there?" Con hissed, spotting her on his tactical display.

She was paired with Archon, so I agreed it made no sense. However, we had a tight window, forcing us to follow it to achieve our objectives.

"Stick to the plan," I reminded him. "They've got their directives; we've got ours."

Con hesitated, then nodded. We continued toward the main building, using the distraction to our advantage.

The guards had rushed to respond to the breach, leaving our path temporarily clear.

The interior was stark and utilitarian—polished concrete floors, reinforced walls, and surveillance cameras at every junction. We disabled the cameras as we progressed, moving deeper into the complex until we reached a secured laboratory.

The electronic lock on the lab entryway proved more challenging than expected. Three failed attempts would trigger a silent alarm. I connected my decryption module and ran through the bypass sequences, sweat beading on my forehead as the seconds ticked by.

"Hurry," Con urged, keeping watch behind us.

"Almost..." The lock finally yielded, flashing green after a complex sequence of cryptographic exchanges. "Got it."

The portal slid open, revealing a cavernous space filled with servers, workstations, and at its center, a device unlike anything I'd ever seen. It resembled an MRI machine but with additional components that gave it an ominous appearance.

"The pulse weapon prototype," Con confirmed, his voice low.

I moved to the nearest terminal and connected my access module. The system requested an authentication, and I spotted the Metzger handshake protocol McLaren had mentioned. The revelation chilled me a second time—how could she have known?

I bypassed the authentication and began extracting data, scanning through the files as they downloaded.

"I've found something," I said, pointing at the screen. "It's not just an EMP. There's an integration between the AI targeting system and neural interface technology."

Con leaned closer, his shoulder touching mine. "Making it selectively affect certain targets?"

"Yes, but there's more." I scrolled through the technical specifications that made my blood run cold. "The neural interface component allows them to exempt specific individuals from the effects. I've never seen anything like this architecture before."

Our faces were so close that I could feel his breath on my cheek. For a moment, the mission faded into the background, and I was acutely aware of him—his scent, his warmth, and the intensity in his eyes as they met mine. I couldn't allow myself to consider what life would be like without him. Every mission was that dangerous. Lives were lost. People came home in boxes.

"Lex," he said, my name barely a whisper on his lips.

I swallowed, forcing myself back to the task at hand. "We need to gather all the data we can," I said, my voice steadier than I felt. "This technology could be devastating in the wrong hands."

Con's eyes lingered on mine a beat longer than necessary before he turned to scan the room for additional storage drives or backup systems.

I continued the download, monitoring the progress bar while trying to quiet the hammering of my heart.

The sound of footsteps approaching cut our mission short. "We've got company," Con warned.

I hastily disconnected my module, the data extraction at eighty-seven percent. "We need to find another way out."

Con pointed to the maintenance access along the far wall. "There. Service corridors run throughout."

We removed the panel and slipped into a narrow passage just as the laboratory door opened. Through a small gap, I caught a glimpse of armed guards sweeping the room, their weapons at the ready.

Con led the way, our progress slow in the confined space. The walls pressed in on all sides, and pipes ran along the ceiling, forcing us to hunch as we moved.

"Wait," I whispered, stopping suddenly. "Listen."

Shots erupted from somewhere nearby—sharp, staccato bursts echoing in the metal structure. We continued navigating the maze of service tunnels, using Con's tactical display to orient ourselves toward the source of the gunfire. The sounds grew louder as we approached, interspersed with shouted commands in Russian.

When we emerged into a hallway near the eastern wing, the air was thick with smoke, and bullet holes scarred the walls. Following the trail of destruction, we reached an area that resembled a firing range.

Bennett was there, slumped against a wall, blood seeping through his tactical vest. Dr. McLaren crouched nearby, her face pale with shock.

"What happened?" Con demanded, kneeling to examine Bennett's wound.

"Ambush," Bennett gasped. "Orlov was waiting for us."

McLaren's voice was shaky. "He knew exactly where we'd be. We need to move, now."

I caught her eye, searching for any sign of deception, but her expression revealed only fear and tension. Still, something felt off. The way she'd known about the Metzger firewalls. How she avoided my gaze now. More, she was supposed to be with Archon, and Bennett with Renegade. Where were they?

"Can you walk?" Con asked Bennett, helping him to his feet.

Bennett nodded grimly, leaning heavily on Con. "This exit is compromised," he said through gritted teeth. "We need another way out."

"The service passageways," I suggested, taking point. "I'll lead. This way."

We retreated into the maintenance tunnels, me in front, Con supporting Bennett, and McLaren bringing up the rear. The narrow space hampered our movement, with Bennett's injury further slowing our progress.

The alarm systems continued to wail as we navigated the service network. Twice, we had to freeze in place as their teams passed by the access areas.

"How much farther?" McLaren whispered, her voice tight with tension.

"Almost there," I replied. "The northwestern perimeter has fewer guards. We can exit there."

Bennett's breathing had grown labored, his face slick with sweat. The blood had soaked through his tactical vest, leaving a trail of dark droplets on the metal floor behind us.

"He's fading fast," McLaren observed. "We need to get him out of here."

"We're close," Con assured her, bearing most of Bennett's weight.

We reached an exit point near the perimeter fence. I peered outside, scanning for guards.

"Clear for now," I reported. "But we'll need to move quickly. The fence is thirty meters away."

Con forced the panel open, and we emerged into the cold night air. Searchlights swept the grounds, creating windows of darkness we could use to cross the empty area.

"On my mark," I whispered, watching the lights. "Now!"

We dashed across the expanse, Con half carrying Bennett while McLaren and I provided cover. The fence loomed before us, its electrified wires humming with a lethal current. Con attached a device to it that created a temporary dead zone in the electrical system.

"Hurry," he urged as he cut a gap. "This will only work for twenty seconds."

We helped Bennett through, then followed quickly, sealing the breach behind us. We made it to our extraction vehicle without further incident, though every shadow seemed to conceal potential threats.

As we sped away from the compound with Dr. McLaren behind the wheel, I watched Bennett in the dim light of the cab. Despite his injury, his eyes remained alert, calculating. There was none of the disorientation or shock typical of a man who'd lost as much blood as he had.

Con applied a field dressing to Bennett's wound. "The bullet passed through cleanly," he reported. "But we need to get you properly treated soon."

Bennett nodded, his jaw tight with pain—or perhaps something else. "Did you get what we came for?"

"Enough to understand what we're dealing with," Con confirmed.

The rest of the journey passed in tense silence, each of us lost in our own thoughts.

The safe house felt exposed, though we'd swept it for bugs upon our return. Bennett's wound had been properly dressed, and he rested on the sofa in the main room, refusing to be confined to a bedroom.

"What's our next move?" McLaren asked.

Con spread a map on the table, his expression unreadable. "We analyze what we've learned and plan our next approach."

"There's no time for that," Bennett insisted, checking his mobile. "We need to relocate. Soon. They'll find us here."

"How?" Con asked, his tone casual, but his eyes sharp.

Bennett's jaw tightened. "Orlov has resources we can't match."

McLaren sat silently by the window, her attention seemingly focused on the street outside. I watched her reflection in the glass, noting how her eyes occasionally flicked to Bennett.

Con marked the installation schematic with our infiltration points. "Interesting that the alarm triggered exactly where you two entered," he observed, his tone neutral.

Before either Bennett or McLaren could respond, Renegade and Archon walked in. Based on the looks on their faces, both were fit to be tied. "I'll deal with them," I told Con before leading the two operatives into another room. "What happened?" I asked, looking between them.

"Once we split up from you and Con, Bennett said he was switching things up. He told us to continue to the western perimeter while he and Dr. McLaren inspected the testing location," Renegade reported.

"He pulled rank," Archon added. "We heard the gunfire, but by the time we reached the main building, you were pulling out."

"Copy that," I responded. Bennett was becoming more of a problem with every passing minute. And, given I outranked him, it was time I set things straight. "Wait here," I said, returning to the other room.

"If you have something to say, Infidel, say it directly," Bennett said when I returned.

"Noting facts," Con replied evenly.

"This is absurd," Bennett growled. "We were the ones who took fire."

"Yes," I said, studying him. "After disregarding a direct order."

He raised a brow. "I did no such thing."

"You and Renegade were to report to the testing field. According to him, you ordered him to proceed west with Archon instead."

"The teams made no sense. Neither of those two have the experience to evaluate the testing site while Dr. McLaren and I do."

I shook my head. "The time to address the change was prior to the start of the op. You were out of line, doing so once we were in position. Not only that, but you were not authorized to use nonstandard ammunition rounds for a standard infiltration."

Something dangerous flickered in Bennett's eyes. "There are aspects of this operation you're not privy to."

"What did you say?" I tried to keep my tone even, but the rage I felt was still apparent.

The tension in the room thickened, the air between us charged with unspoken accusations. I shifted slightly, positioning myself where I could react if the situation deteriorated. "This isn't your fucking mission, Malcolm, and I resent—"

McLaren rested her hand on my arm and cleared her throat. "This hostility isn't productive. We need to focus on what matters—the data you recovered."

"Agreed," said Con as our gazes met.

"*I'll* handle the technical analysis," I said, looking between McLaren and Bennett.

"Of course," she replied. "But if you need assistance…"

"I'll let you know," I finished.

As the night progressed, Con and I studied what we'd recovered.

"These targeting capabilities," I murmured to Con when we were alone in the bedroom. "They could disable critical infrastructure while leaving their own systems intact."

Con's expression remained stoic, but I could read the concern in his eyes. "We need to formulate a response based on this intelligence," he replied, steeling his expression. "Tomorrow will be crucial."

When we returned to the main room, Bennett was watching us intently. "Well?"

"It's as we feared," Con replied. "But the intel gives us what we need to mount a decisive operation. Therefore, I agree we should move against Orlov tomorrow."

Bennett nodded, satisfied. "Good. I'll be ready."

"Your wound—" McLaren began.

"Won't slow me down," Bennett cut her off.

As the safe house settled, Con assigned watch rotations. Tag and I took the first shift, positioned by the window where we could monitor both the street outside and the room behind me.

The quiet hours of my watch stretched endlessly, filled with unanswered questions that multiplied with each passing minute. Why had the alarm triggered at Bennett and McLaren's position? How had McLaren known details about systems she shouldn't have? And why did Bennett seem so insistent on moving forward despite his injury?

When Archon relieved me, I returned to the bedroom and found Con still awake.

"I'm worried."

He looked up at me. "I'd ask what about, but the end of the world seems cause enough."

I half smiled. "Were McLaren's and Bennett's actions today based on the misinformation you put in their briefs?"

"I've been thinking about that too. Not precisely enough to say with certainty. However, that they're sharing information with each other is evident. Then again, we're all working the same mission, so that they are, isn't damning in itself."

"Any leaks otherwise?" I asked.

Con shook his head and motioned for me to join him. Our eyes met before I rested my head on his chest. In his, I saw the same terror I felt over what we were up against.

21

Con

I watched Lex through the darkness of our room, her face illuminated by the glow of her tablet as she analyzed the data we'd gathered. Neither of us had found sleep after discovering Bennett's deception and McLaren's suspicious knowledge of Orlov's systems. Despite the exhaustion weighing on my limbs, my mind refused to quiet.

An alert from Kestrel appeared on my phone. *No word on Nightingale. Chatter suggests full-scale demo eleven hundred tomorrow. Multiple hostiles to attend.*

I raised my head, and my eyes met Lex's. "It's on."

"When?"

I read Kestrel's message aloud.

"We need to move on this immediately," said Lex.

"Agreed." I pushed myself off the bed where I'd been reviewing surveillance images. "Let's gather the team."

We found Tag in the kitchen, cleaning his weapon.

"Time to earn our keep," I told him. "Confirmed intelligence on Orlov's demonstration. Tomorrow morning."

His brow furrowed. "Copy that. I'll wake Renegade and Archon."

Within twenty minutes, our makeshift command center buzzed with activity. Bennett arrived last, his complexion ashen, the bandage on his shoulder spotted with fresh blood. Despite his injury from yesterday's mission, determination blazed in his eyes.

McLaren took one look at him and shook her head. "Malcolm, you need medical attention—"

"I'm fine," he spat, though his labored breathing suggested otherwise.

Lex stood beside me when I spread the facility schematics across the central table, drawing the team's attention to our target. "Everyone clear on their positions?" I surveyed the faces around me. Tag's expression remained stoic, while Renegade and Archon acknowledged my question with "yes, sirs."

"We have a tight window," I continued, marking the entry points on the digital map. "After that, Labyrinth goes from theoretical threat to active weapon."

"The stakes couldn't be higher," Lex added, her voice steady despite the pressure crushing down on us all. "If Orlov completes this demonstration, there's no putting this technology back in the box."

Bennett shifted uncomfortably in his chair, wincing as the movement disturbed his wound.

"Malcolm, I'm pulling you from the op," Lex said before I had the chance to say it myself.

"The hell you are," he snapped. "You can't go in there without me. I made sure of it."

"What in the bloody hell does that mean?" I barked.

"I told you there were things you weren't privy to. Either you take me with you, or you'll have no way to stop the demonstration."

"I'll see to it this ends your career," Lex seethed.

Bennett's expression was chilling. "It's already over, Dr. Sterling."

"We can't risk it," warned McLaren. "We need to stop Orlov at all costs. Whether Malcolm is bluffing or not isn't something to chance."

"Fine," I relented, knowing further argument would waste precious time. I turned to Bennett. "You're with Archon on the east approach. Minimal resistance expected there."

Bennett's eyes narrowed, but he offered no protest.

I outlined the final plan and assigned positions. "Tag and Renegade, you'll take the south entrance. Lex and I will approach from the west—likely the heaviest resistance, but also the most direct path to the demonstration area."

"What about me?" McLaren asked.

"You'll coordinate from here," I replied. "Your expertise in neural interfaces means you can guide us once we're inside. If we encounter technical obstacles, we'll need your knowledge."

She accepted this with a short nod, though something flickered behind her eyes—something I didn't like. I pressed on anyway.

"Once inside, our primary objective is to reach the central laboratory and disable the neural interface," I continued. "Secondary objective is Orlov himself. Questions?"

No one spoke. The gravity of our mission had sobered all of us.

"Departure in thirty minutes," I concluded. "Gear up."

As the team dispersed to make the final preparations, Lex stayed behind, her fingers tracing the facility layout on the display.

"We're missing something," she murmured, too low for the others to hear.

I leaned closer. "What do you mean?"

"The intelligence is too clean, too complete." Her brow furrowed. "It's as if someone wanted us to have this information."

"A trap?"

"Or a test." She met my gaze, her dark eyes reflecting my own concerns. "Either way, we need to proceed."

I touched her arm gently. "Stay close to me in there."

"Roger that," she replied, the two words carrying a weight beyond their syllables.

As darkness cloaked our approach, we moved toward Orlov's compound. Our team split into three groups, each taking different entry points to minimize the detection risk. Tactical vests equipped with limited comms kept us connected as we penetrated the outer perimeter.

Lex moved beside me, her breathing steady despite the tension.

"In position," Tag's voice murmured through my earpiece.

"East team ready," came Bennett's confirmation.

I glanced at Lex, who gave a brief affirmative gesture. "West team proceeding," I responded. "Execute on my mark."

The facility loomed ahead, its security more fortified than our previous infiltration had revealed. New motion sensors dotted the fence line, and additional guards patrolled in tighter rotations. Orlov had clearly anticipated our return.

"Three…two…one…mark," I whispered.

We breached the perimeter simultaneously, our coordinated approach designed to overwhelm their security response. For precious seconds, everything proceeded according to plan—until floodlights blazed to life across the compound.

"They were waiting for us," Lex hissed as guards emerged from concealed positions.

Gunfire erupted from multiple directions. Not random suppression—targeted shots from trained personnel who knew exactly where we'd be. Our plan had been compromised.

"Fall back to the secondary positions," I ordered through the comms, pulling Lex behind a storage container as bullets peppered the ground where we'd stood.

No response came through the channel. Either our comms had been jammed, or the others couldn't reply. Either way, we were isolated.

"We need to reach the main laboratory," Lex said, checking her weapon.

"No doubt they've accelerated the timeline."

More guards converged on our position, forcing us to retreat farther from our planned route. Each exchange of gunfire drove us deeper into the facility and farther from the area where Orlov would be conducting his demonstration.

"This way," I urged, spotting the maintenance access we used yesterday.

We slipped through the narrow passage, the sounds of pursuit temporarily fading behind us.

"We need to hurry," said Lex, racing ahead of me.

"*Wait—*"

An explosion rocked the facility, the concussion wave nearly throwing us off our feet. Alarms blared as emergency lighting switched on, bathing everything in pulsing red.

"That came from the east entrance," I noted grimly. "Bennett and Archon's position."

Lex's expression tightened. "We need to keep moving."

We navigated through increasingly unfamiliar passages, guided more by instinct than intel. Another explosion, closer this time, sent debris raining from the ceiling. The facility was under attack—but from whom?

As we rounded a corner, three guards appeared, weapons raised. I fired first, dropping two while Lex eliminated the third. We claimed their access badges, hoping they might grant us entry to restricted areas.

"The main laboratory is one level down," said Lex.

We located a stairwell and descended, the sounds of conflict intensifying above us. At the bottom, an armored door stood between us and the laboratory complex. I swiped one of the confiscated badges, but the reader flashed red.

"Higher clearance required," Lex muttered, examining the lock. "I can override it, but I'll need time."

"Which we don't have," I replied, eyeing the corridor behind us. "Step back."

I planted a small breaching charge on the electronic lock, using our bodies as shields when it detonated. The door's mechanism failed, allowing us to force it open manually.

Beyond lay a transitional space—an antechamber leading to multiple laboratory wings. The central display indicated active testing outside, with power consumption spiking to unprecedented levels in a lab different than where we were previously.

"That's our target," I confirmed, checking my weapon's magazine.

"Con," Lex gripped my arm, her expression grave. "Whatever happens in there—"

"We come back out together," I finished for her.

She squeezed my hand once, then we moved toward the lab, flanking its entrance. Through the reinforced glass panels, I glimpsed a central apparatus glowing with blue-white energy. In the control booth above, monitors displayed what appeared to be targeting data.

I tried my comm unit one final time. "All teams, report position." Only static answered.

"Ready?" I asked Lex.

She exhaled steadily. "Now."

We burst through the doors, weapons raised, but the place was empty. At the center of the room stood the neural interface device.

"We need to stop the test sequence!" Lex shouted, advancing toward the main control console.

A gunshot rang out, the bullet striking the floor near my feet. I spun toward the source and froze.

Bennett stood with his weapon trained not on me, but on Lex. His arm encircled her throat, the barrel of his pistol pressed against her temple.

"Don't move, Carnegie," he called out, his voice eerily calm. "Not if you want her to live."

McLaren emerged from behind the neural interface, tablet in hand. "This isn't what you think, Infidel."

"What have you done?" I gasped.

Bennett's expression was sinister. "What was necessary."

"Put down your weapon," McLaren instructed, her tone that of a professor addressing a wayward student. "Please don't force Malcolm to hurt her."

I assessed our options, finding none that guaranteed Lex's safety. Slowly, I lowered my weapon to the ground.

"Kick it away," Bennett ordered.

I complied, watching it skid across the polished floor.

"Now, step away from the console."

As I moved back, McLaren approached, her attention divided between me and the neural interface, which continued its ominous power build.

"You're working with Orlov," I said, the betrayal bitter in my mouth.

"I've been working with Viktor for twenty years," McLaren corrected, reaching the control station. "Since long before either MI6 or Unit 23 understood what we were developing."

"You led us here," Lex said, her voice taut as she remained in Bennett's grip. "The entire operation was a setup."

Bennett's laugh held no warmth. "Not initially. We needed to monitor your progress, keep you chasing shadows while we completed the final phase."

"But your expertise became essential when we encountered integration issues," McLaren added, fingers moving across the control surface. "The defensive algorithms wouldn't stabilize."

"Defensive?" I challenged. "You're building a weapon of mass disruption."

"It was never meant to be a weapon!" McLaren's voice rose with unexpected passion. "The neural interface was designed as a shield—a way to protect essential infrastructure during conflicts while allowing targeted, minimal force against military objectives."

"Targeted weapons still kill people," Lex countered.

"Fewer than conventional warfare," Bennett retorted. "*That* was the original intent—precision that would minimize civilian casualties."

McLaren's expression darkened. "Until Viktor saw the true potential. Not just acting as a shield, but actively targeting whatever anyone wanted. Beyond military communications, power grids, hospital systems, and air traffic control—anything with an electronic signature."

"Mass devastation," I concluded.

Bennett's grip on Lex tightened. "We discovered his plans eight months ago. Evidence of contracted attacks against sixteen nations simultaneously—enough to trigger global chaos and allow certain interests to consolidate power."

"So you've been trying to stop him?" Lex asked, disbelief evident in her tone.

"We needed access to the core programming," McLaren explained, her fingers still working at the console. "But Viktor compartmentalized everything after he realized we had doubts."

"The threats against you at Blackmoor," Bennett continued. "We orchestrated them, trying to separate you from Carnegie. We needed your expertise without drawing attention to our involvement."

"You're saying you're the good guys?" I scoffed, inching imperceptibly closer.

"We didn't have a choice!" McLaren snapped. "Viktor is activating the system today. If we don't complete the countermeasure algorithm, millions will die when he demonstrates its 'limited capabilities' to his financial backers."

"And you need Lex because?" I pressed, gauging the distance between us.

"It takes two people to complete the countermeasures and sabotage the entire system," McLaren explained, desperation edging into her voice. "One to stabilize the neural mapping while another corrupts the targeting parameters. I can't do it alone."

"You expect us to trust you?" Lex demanded, still struggling against Bennett's grip.

"You don't have to trust us," Bennett replied. "But if you want to stop Orlov, you need us."

A new alarm sounded—more urgent, more final than those still blaring throughout the facility.

"He's here," McLaren whispered, her face paling. "Viktor is initiating the final preparations."

Bennett's attention wavered for a fraction of a second—enough for Lex to drive her elbow into his solar plexus. As he doubled over, gasping, she twisted free, ducking low as his weapon discharged wildly.

I lunged forward and retrieved my sidearm. Before I could aim, the laboratory doors burst open and Orlov entered, flanked by at least a dozen armed operatives in tactical gear.

"Evelyn," the Russian scientist called, his gaunt face registering surprise rather than alarm. "What is happening here?"

"System diagnostics," McLaren answered smoothly, her fingers never pausing on the console. "Final calibrations before your demonstration."

Orlov's eyes narrowed as he surveyed the room, taking in Bennett's disheveled appearance, Lex's defensive stance, and my retrieved weapon.

"I see," he said quietly. "You've brought friends."

In an instant, the laboratory erupted into chaos. Orlov's men opened fire, forcing us to dive for cover behind equipment banks. Bullets ricocheted off metal surfaces, shattering monitors.

"Lex!" I shouted, unable to see her through the melee.

"The console!" McLaren's voice cut through the gunfire. *"Margot, we need to complete the counter-measure now!"*

I provided covering fire, dropping two of Orlov's men as they tried to flank our position. Through gaps in the equipment, I glimpsed Lex making her way toward McLaren.

"Bennett!" I called. "Cover their position!"

For a moment, I thought he would refuse—that his earlier performance had revealed his true allegiance. Then he pivoted, laying down suppressive fire that allowed Lex to reach McLaren's side.

"What do I need to do?" Lex demanded, taking position at the adjacent terminal.

"Initialize the secondary protocol while I stabilize the primary matrix," McLaren instructed, her professional composure returning despite the bullets flying around them.

Orlov shouted orders in Russian, directing his remaining forces to converge on them. I shifted position, drawing their fire toward me instead of the women working frantically to stop his weapon.

Bennett's earlier tension appeared to vanish as he called out to me. "When they finish, get them out through the maintenance tunnels. Section J-7 connects to the exterior."

Before I could respond, Bennett broke from cover, advancing toward Orlov's position. His sudden movement drew concentrated fire, but he continued forward, absorbing multiple hits without faltering.

"Malcolm, no!" McLaren cried, looking up from her work.

Bennett ignored her, his focus locked on Orlov, who had retreated behind his security detail. With a final burst of strength, Bennett broke through their line, shooting the Russian scientist before tackling him to the ground.

Two shots echoed above the general cacophony. Bennett's body went rigid, then slumped forward atop Orlov. Blood pooled beneath them as the remaining guards hesitated, momentarily shocked by their employer's demise.

I used the distraction to reach Lex and McLaren. "How much longer?"

"Almost there," Lex replied. "The countermeasure is uploading."

Orlov's men regrouped and, rather than help their fallen leader, advanced on our position. I fired until my magazine emptied, then drew my backup weapon.

"Done!" McLaren announced, initiating the final sequence. "The neural interface is rejecting Orlov's targeting parameters."

On the main display, warning indicators flashed as the system began destabilizing. The blue-white energy at the core of the device pulsed erratically, power fluctuations cascading through the connected systems.

"It's overloading," Lex warned, reading the diagnostic output. "The countermeasure is triggering a chain reaction in the power core. This place is going to blow!"

I pulled Lex away from the console. *"We need to move. Now!"*

McLaren hesitated, looking toward Bennett's motionless form. "We can't leave him—"

"He's gone," I said firmly, grabbing her arm.

As warning lights flashed across every monitor, Lex gripped Evelyn's arm. *"Are you Janus?"* she shouted.

As McLaren jerked from Lex's grasp, her face revealed nothing—not surprise, not confusion, not recognition—just a blank stare amidst the chaos surrounding us.

The first explosion came from the power coupling nearest the neural interface. Equipment racks toppled as ceiling panels crashed down. Orlov's remaining men fled, abandoning their fallen leader amid the destruction.

"Let her go!" I shouted at Lex when McLaren took off in the opposite direction.

We kept going until we reached a junction where the tunnel split in three directions. Behind us, the laboratory was now fully engulfed in flames as secondary explosions drove us forward.

We went right, traveling twenty meters, when the largest explosion yet rocked the building. The tunnel's ceiling collapsed behind us, cutting off our retreat. Worse, the shock wave hurled debris forward, striking Lex and sending her sprawling. Blood streamed from a gash on her forehead, and her breathing came in labored gasps.

"Leave me," she insisted, pushing weakly at my hands. "I'll only slow you down."

"The hell I will." I lifted her into my arms and ran through the increasingly unstable passage, dust and small debris raining down with each new explosion that shook the compound above. The tunnel began to slope upward, suggesting we were nearing an exit.

"There!" Lex pointed to a maintenance hatch ahead, pale light visible through its grille.

"Can you stand?" I asked, knowing I'd need both hands to get us out.

"Put me down!" she shouted, working the mechanism before I had the chance to. The hatch released with a metallic groan, revealing the predawn sky above.

We'd barely cleared the immediate blast radius when another explosion, larger than any before, tore through the complex. The concussive force threw us forward, debris raining down around us.

I turned to shield Lex with my body, protecting her from the worst of it. Pain lanced through my side as something struck me—once, twice—driving the breath from my lungs.

When the immediate danger passed, I tried to straighten, but found I couldn't. My vision swam, darkness encroaching at the edges.

"Con?" Lex's voice sounded distant. *"Con!"*

I felt her hands on me, rolling me onto my back. The sky above spun lazily, stars visible despite the flames illuminating the destruction behind us.

"You're hit," she said, her voice breaking as she pressed against my side. Her hands came away red. "Stay with me, Con. Help will come," she said, tearing fabric from her shirt to shove against my wound.

The pain receded, replaced by a spreading coldness that should have concerned me more than it did. My thoughts became sluggish, disconnected.

"Lex," I whispered, reaching for her. My fingers left a smear of blood on her cheek as I traced its curve. "I need to tell you—"

"Don't you dare," she interrupted, tears cutting tracks through the dust on her face. "Save it for when you're recovered."

I smiled, or tried to. "Just in case...I love you, Margot Sterling."

Her face blurred before me, my consciousness fading despite her desperate pleas to stay awake. The last thing I saw was her eyes, fierce and determined, refusing to let me go as darkness claimed me.

22

Lex

The world compressed to a single focus: Con's blood seeping between my fingers as I applied pressure to his wound. His final words before losing consciousness echoed in my head. *I love you, Margot Sterling.*

"Stay with me," I pleaded, cradling his head. "Don't you dare leave me now."

The wail of approaching sirens pierced the predawn air. Help was coming, but Con's breathing had grown shallow, his pulse weak beneath my trembling fingers. The explosion that had destroyed Orlov's facility continued to send debris raining down around us, but I couldn't move—wouldn't move—from Con's side.

Medical personnel swarmed us within minutes, their voices clipped and efficient as they assessed his injuries.

"Multiple traumas, possible internal bleeding," one paramedic reported.

"BP dropping," another called out.

They worked with practiced coordination, stabilizing him for transport. I rose on unsteady legs, refusing to be separated from him.

"I'm coming with him," I stated when they loaded him into the ambulance.

The paramedic glanced at my bloodstained clothes and the gash on my forehead. "You need medical attention too, ma'am."

"I'll get it at the hospital."

As the ambulance raced toward the nearest trauma center, I held Con's hand, willing strength into him with each squeeze. The vehicle's motion blurred with the turmoil in my mind. Dr. McLaren—my mentor, my guide for the past decade—had been involved with Labyrinth from the beginning. The revelation cut deeper than any physical wound.

At the hospital, they whisked Con away to surgery, leaving me in a stark waiting area. A nurse led me to an examination room where a doctor cleaned and stitched the gash on my forehead, pronouncing me lucky to have escaped with minor injuries.

"Your colleague wasn't as fortunate," she said. "The surgical team is working on him now."

I thanked her mechanically, then returned to the waiting area, unable to focus on anything but the clock on the wall marking each excruciating minute Con spent in surgery.

Three hours later, Tag found me there, his face grim with fatigue and worry.

"Any word?" he asked, dropping into the chair beside me.

I shook my head, not trusting my voice.

"The team is safe," he reported. "Renegade took a hit, but nothing critical."

"What about Archon?"

"He's been knocked out by the thugs helping Bennett, as was Renegade, but otherwise, uninjured."

I nodded, grateful for the news but unable to feel true relief while Con's fate remained uncertain.

"McLaren?" I finally asked.

"Uncertain." Tag's eyes hardened. "They're still sifting through the rubble. At this point, it's considered recovery, not rescue."

My stomach twisted. "And Orlov?"

"Alive, barely. We extracted him before the main explosion. He's in surgery now." Tag's voice dropped lower. "Bennett was DOA."

I closed my eyes, recalling Bennett's final charge toward Orlov. Whatever his motives, his sacrifice had given us the chance to stop the demonstration.

"What happened in there, Lex?"

I told him everything—McLaren's betrayal, Bennett's revelation about their true mission, the countermeasure they claimed to have implemented.

"So McLaren helped create Labyrinth, then tried to sabotage it when she realized Orlov's true intentions?" Tag summarized.

"That's what she claimed," I replied. "But I don't know what to believe anymore. The woman I thought I knew would never have helped create something so dangerous in the first place."

Tag's hand rested on my shoulder. "The best lies contain elements of truth. Maybe she convinced herself she was doing the right thing."

A surgeon approached before I could respond. I stood so quickly the room tilted.

"He's stabilized," the doctor announced. "His major organs are intact, but he lost a significant amount of blood. We've repaired the damage, but the next twenty-four hours will be critical."

Relief washed over me, leaving my knees weak. "Can I see him?"

"He's in recovery now. Once he's moved to intensive care, you can visit briefly."

Two more hours passed before a nurse led me to Con's room. The sight of him, pale and still among the machines monitoring his vital signs, nearly undid me. I sank into the chair beside his bed, taking his hand in mine.

"You promised we'd come out together," I whispered. "I'm holding you to that."

His fingers remained limp in mine, but the steady beep of the heart monitor offered reassurance that he was fighting. I settled in to wait, refusing offers of food or rest.

As the day faded, nurses came and went, checking his vital signs and adjusting the medications. I remained a fixture at his bedside, unwilling to leave even for a moment.

Near midnight, his fingers twitched in mine. I straightened, watching his face for any sign of consciousness.

"Con?" I leaned closer, hope swelling in my chest.

His eyelids fluttered, then opened. Disorientation clouded his gaze before focusing on me.

"Lex," he whispered, his voice a dry rasp.

I reached for the cup of ice chips the nurse had left, spooning a few into his mouth. "Don't try to talk too much. You're in hospital. The surgery went well."

He swallowed, grimacing. "McLaren?"

"We don't know anything yet." I squeezed his hand.

He processed this, then asked, "Orlov?"

"Alive, in surgery last I heard." I stroked his forehead. "Everyone on our team made it out. Other than Bennett, of course." Had he ever been on our team, though? At this point, it no longer mattered.

Relief relaxed his features momentarily before concern returned. "You're hurt." His fingers brushed my bandaged forehead.

"Just a scratch." I caught his hand, pressing it to my cheek. "You're the one who decided to shield me from an explosion."

A ghost of his familiar smirk appeared. "Not my brightest moment."

"It was the bravest, most foolish thing anyone's ever done for me." My voice caught. "I thought I'd lost you."

"I'm harder to kill than that." His eyes searched mine. "Did you hear what I said? Before I passed out?"

I nodded, emotion constricting my throat. "You said you love me."

"I meant it." His gaze held mine, steady despite his weakness.

"I know." I leaned forward, resting my forehead gently against his. "I love you too, Con. I think I have since that first night at Blackmoor, when you showed me who you really are."

His smile was worth every moment of fear and uncertainty I'd endured. "Say it again."

"I love you, Conrad Carnegie," I whispered against his lips. "Don't ever scare me like that again."

"No promises in our line of work," he murmured, "but I'll do my best."

A nurse interrupted our moment, shooing me away while she checked his vitals. I used the break to find Tag in the waiting area and share the news of Con's improvement. Gus and Ash were with him, but when I offered to let them go see him in my place, they declined.

"He needs you now," said Tag.

When I returned, Con was fighting sleep, determined to continue our conversation.

"Any news yet on McLaren?" he asked as I resumed my place beside him.

The wound of her betrayal still felt raw. "None, and honestly, I don't know what to think or even how to feel. For years, she shaped my career, my thinking. Now, I don't know what was real."

Con's fingers found mine. "Her final choice was real. She could have let Labyrinth succeed. Instead, she risked everything to stop it."

"How can you be so sure?" I asked. "Maybe she and Bennett were lying about their motives."

"The countermeasure worked," he pointed out. "The system overloaded instead of launching. Whatever their previous intentions, that final act was one of redemption."

His perspective offered a comfort I hadn't expected. "I still don't know how to reconcile the mentor I knew with the woman who helped create something so deadly."

"People contain multitudes," Con said, his eyes drifting closed despite his efforts. "The McLaren who mentored you was real too."

I stayed awake until his breathing evened into sleep, then curled uncomfortably in the chair beside him, unwilling to leave even for the comfort of a proper bed.

The next days passed in a blur of medical updates and debriefings. Con improved steadily, his natural resilience accelerating his recovery. Mrs. Thorne arrived regularly with both clothing for me and meals for the two of us.

"I don't understand how anyone can recover while eating that ghastly muck they call food around here," she said as she sneaked containers into the room, then served our food on the china she'd brought with her.

I divided my time between his bedside and meetings with MI6 and Unit 23 representatives, piecing together the aftermath of our mission.

Three days after the explosion, Con was scheduled for release when Viper and Typhon arrived for what they called a "comprehensive debrief." The presence of both agency heads in the same room spoke volumes about the significance of what had occurred.

"Orlov survived surgery," Viper reported, her usually composed demeanor showing signs of strain. "So far, he's unable to communicate. However, we have received intel confirming the demonstration was meant to showcase Labyrinth's capabilities to potential buyers."

"Representatives from six nations," Typhon added. "Most unaware of the system's full destructive potential."

Con, sitting up in bed and looking more like himself each hour, frowned. "How did McLaren and Bennett become involved in all this? And why in the bloody hell weren't we briefed on Bennett's Estonia connection to Orlov?"

Viper and Typhon exchanged glances.

"That information was compartmentalized at the highest levels," Typhon admitted. "Bennett's mission in Estonia occurred during a critical period in Russian-Western relations. The details—including his connection to Orlov—were sealed by both govern-ments to prevent a diplomatic fallout."

"So you sent us in blind," I said, anger flaring. "You knew Bennett had history with Orlov but didn't think that warranted disclosure?"

"We did not, Lex. I promise you that," said Viper.

"Unit 23 didn't, either," Typhon added.

"We knew he had expertise," Viper countered, "but the full extent of his involvement with Orlov's research was buried in classified files that even I couldn't access without triggering diplomatic alerts."

"As for Dr. McLaren," Typhon continued, "her role in the original neural interface research was equally obscured. She was recruited for a black-budget proj-ect twenty years ago, before either of us held our current positions."

Con's expression remained skeptical. "And they both managed to maintain their covers all this time?"

"Compartmentalization works both ways," Viper replied. "McLaren was a brilliant researcher, whose contributions to AI ethics were genuine. Her other work remained hidden because no one knew to look for it."

The explanation left me unsatisfied, but arguments wouldn't change what had happened. McLaren's betrayal had permanently altered my worldview, forcing me to question relationships and motivations I'd once taken for granted.

Yet amid this darkness, something unexpected had blossomed. I looked at Con, his strength returning visibly with each passing hour, and recognized that despite everything—or perhaps because of it—I'd found something precious.

"When can we return to Blackmoor?" Con asked, clearly eager to leave the hospital.

"Transport is arranged for this afternoon," Typhon replied. "Assuming the doctor approves your release."

"He will," Con stated with such certainty that even Viper smiled.

After they left, the doctor came in, confirming Con could go home. I helped him dress, ever mindful of his bandaged torso.

"Ready?" I asked, steadying him as he stood.

He looked at me, his eyes searching mine. "Are you coming with me?"

"If you'll have me," I replied, suddenly feeling vulnerable. "I've requested leave from MI6. Viper approved it without question."

Mindful of his wound, Con drew me closer. "I want you at Blackmoor. Not just for a visit."

"I was hoping you'd say that." I rested my head against his chest, listening to the steady beat of his heart. "I'm not ready to be anywhere you're not."

The nurse arrived with the discharge papers and instructions for Con's recovery—demands for rest that I knew he'd ignore as soon as he was back on his feet. By afternoon, we were in a private car, headed to Inverness airport, where Con's pilot waited with the helicopter.

"Good to see you in one piece, sir," Callum greeted us, his Scottish accent more pronounced than most.

"Mostly in one piece," Con replied with a wry smile, his arm around my waist for support as we boarded.

The flight to Blackmoor offered stunning views of the Highland landscape, though Con dozed through most of it, the medications and residual exhaustion claiming him despite his efforts to stay awake. I watched him sleep, still hardly believing we'd both survived.

When we arrived at Blackmoor, I was taken aback to find a welcoming committee gathered at the castle's entrance. Mrs. Thorne stood front and center, flanked by Bastion and the other staff members. Tag waited with Gus, Ash, and Sullivan. Even Ambrose hovered at the edge of the group, his usual distracted demeanor replaced by genuine concern.

Seeing him reminded me of Dr. McLaren's absence. Whatever her role in Labyrinth, she and Ambrose had been close. I wondered what he'd been told, if anything. I still didn't know for certain whether she'd died in the explosion or, like us, had escaped. Another thought lingered. Did Ambrose know about the secret life she'd lived? Had anyone other than Bennett and Orlov?

Con woke as the helicopter landed, looking momentarily disoriented before recognition dawned. "Didn't expect the welcome wagon," he muttered.

"You're loved," I replied simply.

Mrs. Thorne approached first as we disembarked. "Welcome home, my lord." Her eyes glistened with unshed tears as she took in his pale complexion and hesitant movements. "Your rooms are prepared."

"Thank you, Helena." Con's voice carried genuine warmth. "It's good to be here."

The others gathered around, offering support without overwhelming him. Bastion relieved Con of his minimal luggage, while Tag and Ash positioned themselves to assist if needed. Con waved them off, determined to walk under his own power.

"You look like hell," Ash said with a grin that softened the words.

"Better than I feel," Con replied.

As we moved toward the castle entrance, I fell into step beside Ambrose, my curiosity overcoming my hesitation.

"Did you know?" I asked quietly.

Ambrose glanced at me, genuine sorrow in his eyes. "No. Although I sensed she walked a difficult path. But don't we all?"

Before I could press further, we reached the entrance, where Con paused, his strength visibly waning despite his determination.

"Perhaps you should rest before dinner, my lord," Bastion suggested tactfully.

Con nodded, his arm tightening around my waist. "Lex will join me."

No one raised a brow at his pronouncement—further evidence that the castle staff had already accepted what I was only beginning to fully embrace. This was where I belonged now.

As we climbed the stairs to Con's rooms—*our* rooms, I corrected myself—I felt a sense of rightness settle over me. The pain and betrayal of the past week hadn't disappeared, but they existed alongside this new certainty.

Con sank onto the edge of the bed, exhaustion finally claiming him. I knelt to remove his shoes, then helped him lie back against the pillows.

"Stay," he murmured, catching my hand.

I slipped my own shoes off and stretched out beside him, careful not to jostle his wound. His arm curved around me, drawing me against his side.

"We're home," he whispered, his voice already thick with the approaching sleep.

As Con's breathing deepened, I gazed around the room that would now be mine as well. The ancient castle walls had witnessed centuries of Carnegie history, and now, I would become part of that lineage—not through marriage, at least not yet, but through a bond forged in danger and sealed by choice.

Blackmoor called to something in me, just as Con did. The strength, the history, the sense of belonging—all things I'd sought throughout my life without recognizing them. Here, I could be both the MI6 analyst and the woman who had found love when she least expected it.

I nestled closer to Con, listening to his heartbeat beneath my ear. Whatever challenges lay ahead—and there would be many, including the lingering questions about McLaren's fate—we would face them together. I had found my place, and it was here, within these ancient walls, with him.

23

Con

Two weeks after the destruction of Orlov's facility, I stood at my bedroom window, watching the Highland mist roll across the grounds of Blackmoor. Spring was showing its first signs, bringing new growth to the ancient estate, though my body still ached from the wounds I'd sustained.

The doctor had prescribed six weeks of rest, a directive I'd been fighting since the moment I regained consciousness. Lex, however, proved more formidable than any physician. Her stern glances and gentle insistence had kept me relatively compliant, though I'd compromised on my working from bed rather than the ops hub.

"Coffee?" Lex appeared in the doorway, balancing a tray with two steaming cups.

"God, yes." I turned from the window, admiring how at home she looked in my—our—bedroom. She wore one of my jumpers over her trousers, the sleeves rolled up to her wrists, her dark hair pulled back in a loose knot.

She set the tray on the bedside table and pressed her palm to my forehead. "No fever. That's good."

"I told you I was fine."

"The same way you told me you were 'fine' when you were bleeding internally?" Her tone was light, but I caught the shadow that crossed her face whenever she referenced those harrowing moments.

I cupped her cheek. "I'm here. I'm not going anywhere."

She leaned into my touch. "You'd better not."

The domesticity that had developed between us over the past fortnight still astonished me. Lex had slipped into my life at Blackmoor as though she'd always belonged here—charming my staff and transforming my bedroom into a functional workspace when I insisted on reviewing intelligence reports despite her objections.

We took our cups to the sitting area by the fireplace, where I'd been reviewing the latest reports on Orlov. My muscles protested as I lowered myself on the sofa, a reminder that my recovery remained incomplete.

"You're overdoing it," Lex observed, curling up beside me.

"I've been sitting for hours. Walking to the window hardly counts as exertion."

She raised a brow. "Those stairs to the battlements yesterday?"

"Needed fresh air."

"And the inspection of the east wing renovations the day before?"

I grinned. "Architectural interest."

"Stubborn man." Her fond exasperation warmed me more than my coffee.

"You knew that when you agreed to stay."

"I did," she conceded. "Though I expected at least a pretense of following medical advice."

Before I could counter, Bastion appeared in the doorway. "Lord Blackmoor, your guests have arrived."

"Show them into the upstairs drawing room, please."

Minutes later, we entered the room filled with the familiar voices of Tag, Ash, Sullivan, and Gus. The sight of them—my closest friends, my brothers in all but blood—brought a sense of completion to my recovery that medicine couldn't provide.

"You're looking less corpse-like," Tag observed, dropping into a chair without waiting for an invitation.

"Charming as ever," I replied.

Gus approached more cautiously, eyeing my bandaged torso visible beneath my unbuttoned shirt. "How's the wound?"

"Healing. Doctor says another month before I'm cleared for field work."

"Which he's already ignoring," Lex added, accepting a hug from Sullivan.

"Of course he is," Sullivan said with a knowing smile. "Did you expect anything less?"

"I live in hope." Lex's dry tone made even Tag chuckle.

As they settled around the room, Mrs. Thorne arrived with refreshments—tea, coffee, and a selection of pastries that reminded me I'd barely touched breakfast.

"So," Ash began once we'd been served. "I assume you want an update?"

I nodded, setting down my cup. "Someone mentioned new information on Orlov."

Gus leaned forward. "The doctors report his cognitive functions are severely compromised. Whether from the bullet wound or some other trauma, he appears unable to communicate beyond basic responses."

"You said 'appears,'" Lex noted.

"It could be an act," Tag concurred. "Though the medical evidence suggests otherwise. Brain scans show damage to his speech centers."

"Convenient," I muttered.

"Very," Ash agreed. "But even if he's faking, the consortium has gone underground. Their financial network has collapsed, and most of their facilities have been abandoned."

"What about McLaren?" Lex's voice remained neutral, but I caught the tension in her shoulders.

A pause stretched between us.

"Still no confirmation," Gus said. "The damage to the facility was extensive. If she was inside during the final explosion…"

He didn't need to finish. We all understood the implications.

Lex's expression remained guarded. I knew she still struggled with McLaren's betrayal, with the knowledge that her mentor had helped create the very weapon we'd risked our lives to destroy. The uncertainty about McLaren's fate only compounded that pain.

"Bennett was officially declared dead," said Gus. "Not that there was a question. However, his body was recovered from the rubble and identified through dental records."

"What about the neural interface technology?" I asked, steering the conversation toward more pragmatic matters.

"Destroyed, as far as we can tell," Ash replied. "The pulse weapon overloaded exactly as McLaren predicted. If any schematics survived, they haven't surfaced."

"We should remain vigilant," I cautioned. "Ideas like that rarely die completely."

"MI6 and Unit 23 have established a joint monitoring program," Lex added. "Any research that bears even a passing resemblance to Orlov's work will trigger alerts."

The conversation drifted to less consequential topics—the latest gossip from Vauxhall Cross, Sullivan's plans for renovations at Ashcroft, and Gus's new financial tracking algorithm. As we talked, I observed the easy camaraderie that had developed between Lex and my friends. She belonged here, among us, in a way that felt both surprising and inevitable.

Eventually, Sullivan announced they needed to leave. "Mairi insisted on serving a special dinner tonight."

"And Ash can't say no," teased Gus.

"The aunt of the Duke of Ashcroft does not intimidate me," Ash protested unconvincingly. "I simply show her the appropriate respect."

Their banter continued as they gathered their things, the normality of it a balm after weeks of intensity. As Gus and Tag prepared to follow them out, I caught Tag's arm.

"Stay a moment?"

He nodded, understanding without an explanation. Lex quietly offered to walk the others out, giving us privacy. Once they'd gone, Tag returned to his chair.

"No word about Nightingale?" I asked, though I already knew the answer.

He shook his head, eyes fixed on the fireplace. "Nothing definitive. There was a possible sighting in Beirut last week, but it went cold."

"You'll find her."

"Will I?" His voice carried a rawness I wasn't accustomed to hearing. "No contact, no trails to follow. She's either dead or doesn't want to be found."

"The fact we haven't found a body gives me hope," Gus offered quietly from the doorway, having returned without Lex, Sullivan, or Ash.

Tag's shoulders tightened. "Or whoever took her ensured there was nothing to find."

"We aren't certain she was taken, Tag," Gus said in a low tone of voice.

The three of us fell silent, each contemplating the grim possibility.

"I'm not giving up," Tag finally said. "Not until she tells me to stop looking."

The fierce determination in his voice revealed more than any confession could have. This wasn't merely professional concern or friendly worry. This was devotion in its purest form.

Gus and I exchanged glances, recognizing what Tag himself might not have yet fully acknowledged. His feelings for Nightingale ran deep—deeper than any of us had realized. What he'd previously described as casual had clearly evolved into something essential.

"We'll help however we can," I promised. "Whatever resources you need."

"We'll find her," Gus added softly. "For all our sakes, but mostly for yours."

Tag looked up, surprise flickering across his features before settling into understanding. He hadn't hidden his feelings as well as he thought.

"We will," he vowed.

After they left, I remained in my chair, contemplating the changes these past months had brought. Before Lex stormed into my castle and hacked my systems, my life had followed a predictable pattern—missions, intelligence gathering, the occasional liaison that never progressed beyond physical attraction. I'd been content with solitude, convinced that deep connections were liabilities in our line of work.

Now, I couldn't imagine returning to that existence. The thought of Blackmoor without Lex's laughter echoing through its halls, without her curious exploration of its secrets, felt hollow beyond bearing.

"You look pensive," Lex observed, returning to find me staring into the fire.

"Thinking about Tag."

She settled beside me. "He's taking Nightingale's disappearance hard."

"Harder than any of us could've predicted. I'm not sure he fully understood his own feelings until she vanished."

"Sometimes, we don't recognize what matters most until it's threatened," she said quietly.

I took her hand, threading our fingers together. "I recognized it the moment you left Blackmoor after our argument. I knew then I couldn't let you go."

Her eyes softened. "Good thing you followed me to London, then."

"Best decision I ever made."

The remainder of the afternoon passed in companionable work—Lex reviewing intelligence reports, me coordinating with various assets who'd been monitoring potential Labyrinth remnants. By evening, we'd established that, while vigilance remained necessary, the immediate threat had dissipated.

"Dinner in an hour," Lex announced, closing her laptop. "Mrs. Thorne mentioned something special."

I smiled, knowing exactly what the "something special" entailed. "Perfect."

While Lex changed into "more appropriate attire," according to her, I messaged Bastion to confirm the final arrangements. Everything was set—the only remaining question was whether I could maintain my composure long enough to surprise her.

An hour later, I led Lex not toward the dining room, but in the direction of the library. She raised a brow but followed without question, her hand warm in mine.

"Where are we going? I thought dinner was—" She stopped as I opened the library doors, revealing the transformation within.

The massive oak table had been cleared of books and papers, replaced by an intimate setting for two. Candles flickered in antique silver holders, casting a warm glow across damask linens and crystal glasses. A fire burned in the hearth, and subtle lighting illuminated the spines of the books lining the walls.

"Con," she breathed, taking in the scene. "What is all this?"

"Dinner," I said, guiding her to the table. "In the place where our journey began."

She looked around, recognition dawning. "Where I first challenged you about Dr. McLaren."

"Where I first realized you might be more than just a temporary alliance."

Bastion appeared with champagne, pouring two glasses before discreetly withdrawing. The first course followed—Mrs. Thorne's signature seafood bisque, a dish she reserved for only the most significant occasions.

"To new beginnings," I proposed, raising my glass.

"And old libraries," Lex added with a smile that reached her eyes.

As we progressed through the meal, our conversation flowed easily, touching on memories of our time together and plans for the future. I found myself entranced by the way the candlelight played across her features, highlighting the intelligence in her dark eyes and the subtle curve of her lips.

When dessert arrived—a chocolate soufflé that Mrs. Thorne had perfected over decades—I knew the moment had come. My heart hammered against my ribs, a reminder of how completely this brilliant, challenging woman had dismantled my defenses.

"Before we finish," I began, my voice steadier than I felt, "there's something I want to say."

Lex set down her spoon, her expression curious.

"When you first arrived at Blackmoor, I saw you as an intrusion. An outsider who represented everything I distrusted about institutional bureaucracy." I smiled at the memory. "I was wrong."

"About the bureaucracy?" she teased.

"About you." I reached across the table, taking her hand. "You challenged me, pushed me to be better. You saw through the walls I spent a lifetime building, and instead of exploiting that vulnerability, you honored it."

Her fingers tightened around mine.

"These past two weeks, even before that, watching you move through Blackmoor as though you've always belonged here, I've realized something profound." I paused, gathering my thoughts. "I don't want to imagine this place—or my life—without you in it."

Understanding dawned in her eyes as I reached into my pocket and withdrew a small velvet box.

"This belonged to my grandmother," I said, opening it to reveal a platinum ring set with a brilliant-cut diamond flanked by rubies. "It's been in the Carnegie family for generations."

I moved to her side, kneeling despite the twinge in my healing wound. "Margot Sterling, will you marry me?"

For a moment, she stared at the ring, her composure giving way to naked emotion. Then her eyes, shining with unshed tears, met mine.

"Yes," she whispered. "Yes, Conrad."

I slipped the ring onto her finger, marveling at how naturally it belonged there. When I rose, she stood with me, her arms encircling my neck as our lips met in a kiss that sealed our promise.

"It's beautiful," she said when we parted, examining the ring in the candlelight.

"It suits you." I brushed a tear from her cheek. "The way it sparkles reminds me of your eyes the first time you challenged me in this very room."

She laughed softly. "I was so determined to dislike you."

"And now?"

"Now, I can't imagine my life without you." She rested her hand against my chest, the ring catching the light. "Though I expect you'll still infuriate me on occasion."

"I'd be disappointed if I didn't." I grinned. "Your mind is never more beautiful than when you're proving me wrong."

Later, as the evening deepened into night, we stood together on the battlements of Blackmoor. The Highland air carried the scent of heather and pine, and stars scattered across the velvet sky.

"What about our careers?" Lex asked, her head resting against my shoulder as we looked out over the moonlit estate. "MI6 and Unit 23 are two entities that don't exactly accommodate married couples."

"We'll make it work," I assured her. "Units have been crossed before, rules bent. And if the institutional constraints become too limiting"—I shrugged—"I've operated independently for years. We could establish our own consultancy."

She considered this. "Partners in every sense."

"Precisely."

"And Blackmoor? Will you want to stay here full time?"

"This is home," I said, gesturing to the ancient stones beneath us. "But it's not the only place we could be. London, Edinburgh, wherever our work takes us— as long as we return here."

She nodded. "It feels right. Coming back to Blackmoor."

"Because it is right." I turned her in my arms, framing her face with my hands. "You belong here, Lex. With me."

Her smile held a certainty that matched my own. "With you," she agreed.

We stayed on the battlements until the cold drove us inside, planning our future amid the stars that had witnessed centuries of Carnegie history. Whatever challenges the remains of Labyrinth might pose, whatever missions might call us away, we would face them with one certainty—we were bound by something stronger than duty or profession. We were bound by love.

As we descended the stone steps, Lex's ring caught the moonlight, sending prisms dancing across the ancient walls. I thought of all the Carnegie brides who had worn it before her, and knew with absolute certainty that none had been more worthy.

Blackmoor had found its countess, and I had found my match.

Epilogue

Lex

The bronze hands of the antique library clock ticked past zero seven hundred hours as I surveyed the newly renovated operations hub beneath Blackmoor Castle. One month had transformed both this space and our lives. Where Con's workstation had once dominated the center, dual command positions now stood as equals.

"Mrs. Thorne outdid herself with breakfast," Con said, entering with two steaming mugs. He moved more fluidly now, his recovery from Inverness nearly complete. Only the occasional stiffness when he reached for something revealed the lingering effects of his wounds.

"You spoil me," I replied, accepting the tea. My engagement ring caught the light as I wrapped my fingers around the mug. I'd learned that six generations of Carnegie brides had worn it before me. The weight of that history had been intimidating at first, but with Con's insistence, I'd finally accepted I belonged here.

"Second thoughts?" he asked, noticing my contemplation of the ring.

"Never." I brushed my lips against his. "Though I'm still adjusting to being called 'countess' by your staff, given I'm not yet."

"Soon enough, my love." His smile reached his eyes in that way that still made my heart skip. "Though none of my ancestors married an MI6 weapons expert."

"Progressive of you."

Con laughed, settling into his chair. "The modifications to the comms array are complete. We're ready for the briefing."

On cue, the lift hummed to life. Moments later, Tag emerged, followed by Gus, Ash, and Sullivan. They'd made this journey from their respective castles for one purpose—Nightingale.

"Good of you to host," Tag said with his customary gruffness.

I activated the main display with a touch. "Before we start, there's something I need to share."

All eyes turned to me as I brought up the forensic data I'd been analyzing for the past fortnight. "None of the remains recovered from Orlov's facility match Dr. McLaren's genetic profile or dental records."

Sullivan leaned forward. "You think she survived?"

"I don't believe we can rule it out." I advanced through several images showing the destruction. "The explosion created multiple exit routes through collapsed walls and ventilation systems. If she knew the facility well enough…"

"She could have escaped during the chaos," Ash finished.

Con's expression remained neutral, though I knew he'd harbored suspicions about McLaren's fate since we discovered the absence of conclusive evidence.

"If she's alive," Gus asked, "whose side is she on?"

A fair question with no simple answer. McLaren had helped create Labyrinth, then claimed to have sabotaged it when she realized Orlov's true intentions. Her final actions had saved countless lives—but her initial choice to develop the technology remained troubling.

"We may never know her true motivations," I admitted. "But we should operate under the assumption she may resurface."

Tag nodded grimly. "Add her to the watch list. Now, about Nightingale…"

He took over the display, bringing up communication intercepts and travel records. "Three sightings in the past week, all in Eastern Europe. The latest puts her in Prague, moving east."

"Voluntary or coerced?" Con asked.

"Unclear." Tag highlighted a surveillance photo—grainy but recognizable as the missing agent. "She appears unrestrained, but there's always someone within five meters of her."

"Handlers," Ash suggested.

Tag agreed. "My assessment as well."

He outlined areas where Nightingale might be headed, based on travel patterns and known safe houses. Throughout his presentation, I watched his face—the contained anguish, the determination.

"I'm proposing a search operation," he concluded. "Small team, minimal footprint. We find her, assess her situation, and extract if needed."

"I'm in," Ash said immediately.

"Count me in for comms support," Sullivan added.

Gus nodded. "I'll handle the financial tracking and transport arrangements."

Con and I exchanged glances, a silent communication that had become second nature.

"Blackmoor's resources are at your disposal," Con stated. "Aircraft, gear, funding—whatever you need. Including the two of us."

"I'll also coordinate with MI6 to ensure you have the proper clearances through the region," I added. "No official involvement, but enough to keep you off watch lists."

Tag's shoulders lowered slightly—the closest he came to displaying relief. "Thank you."

As the meeting progressed into logistical details, Con requested to review the last message supposedly sent from Nightingale. Something about it had troubled him since Tag first mentioned it.

"The wording is odd," Tag explained, sending the text to our screens. "Not her usual syntax."

Con studied it, his brow furrowing. "May I see the encrypted original? Before your systems decoded it?"

Tag transmitted the file. Con ran it through several analysis programs, his focus absolute.

After the team departed with plans to reconvene at Glenshadow the following day, Con remained at his workstation, lost in thought.

"What did you find?" I asked, breaking his concentration.

"Possibly nothing." He highlighted sections of the code. "But there are elements in the encryption that match Kestrel's protocols."

"You think Kestrel sent it?" I studied the pattern-recognition results on the screen.

"Not necessarily." Con leaned back, wincing slightly as he stretched. "But these signature markers are distinctive. Either Kestrel created this message, or…"

His voice trailed off, and I caught a fleeting expression I couldn't quite identify.

"Or?" I prompted.

"Or Nightingale has access to those same methods." Con's eyes met mine, a question lurking in their depths.

I considered the implications. "The timing is curious. Nightingale disappears, then a message arrives with Kestrel's digital fingerprints."

"Coincidences rarely exist in our world," Con murmured, almost to himself, before he switched screens. "It's a loose thread, nothing more. But in our world—"

"Loose threads unravel operations," I finished.

He smiled, reaching for my hand. The simple contact still sent warmth through me. "Time to leave work behind, my love."

"Do we ever?"

He chuckled. "Two peas from the same pod."

We ascended to the main level of Blackmoor, walking in comfortable silence through corridors that had witnessed centuries of Carnegie history. The afternoon light cast long shadows across the Great Hall as we emerged.

"I never properly thanked you," I said as we paused before the massive fireplace.

"For what?"

"For trusting me. From that first night when you showed me your family archives until now." I gestured around us. "You've shared everything—your home, your work, your life."

Con pulled me closer, his arms encircling my waist. "It was the easiest decision I've ever made. And the best."

I leaned into him, savoring the solidity of his presence. "Even if it means following McLaren's ghost?"

"Even then." Con's expression grew serious. "No one from your past or mine will come between what we've built here."

As dusk settled over the Highland landscape, we remained in the Great Hall, planning our role in the search for Nightingale. The castle around us felt more alive than ever—not just with history but with purpose. My life before Blackmoor seemed distant now, as though I'd spent years preparing for a place I hadn't known existed.

I twisted the engagement ring on my finger, marveling at how quickly it had become a part of me. "Do you think we'll find her?"

"Nightingale?" Con considered. "Tag won't stop until he does."

"And McLaren?"

His fingertip traced patterns on my palm. "Some questions remain unanswered. Some people choose to stay in the shadows."

"Like Kestrel?"

He nodded. "Those shadows serve a purpose too."

I pressed my palm against the cool stone wall, feeling the centuries of history beneath my fingertips. Con joined me at the window, his reflection appearing beside mine in the glass. Two people transformed by danger and trust, bound by something few would ever understand.

***

Rain drummed against leaded windows in a London townhouse as twilight descended. In the wood-paneled study, a solitary figure bent over an ancient tome laid open on a mahogany desk. Fingers traced the brittle parchment, where elaborate ink drawings depicted the underground passages beneath the Scottish Highlands.

The leather-bound volume—its spine cracked with age, its pages yellowed by centuries—contained secrets few still remembered. Maps of tunnel networks that ran beneath three Highland estates: Blackmoor, Glenshadow, and Ashcroft.

The figure paused at a section where the tunnels converged, forming what appeared to be a chamber deep underground. A notation in faded ink marked the spot with a symbol that resembled an ouroboros—a serpent consuming its own tail.

The sharp trill of a mobile phone broke the silence.

The figure lifted it without checking the display. "Yes?" The voice was low, measured, revealing neither gender nor emotion.

A muffled voice responded on the other end.

"Yes, it was terribly unfortunate. But we have contingencies." The figure turned a page, revealing more detailed drawings of the tunnel entrances. "Your concern is noted, but the timeline remains unchanged."

Another pause as the caller continued.

"I told you the tunnels are the key." A hint of impatience crept into the otherwise controlled tone. "They always have been. We'll begin phase two immediately."

With a decisive movement, the figure closed the ancient book and slid it into a concealed compartment in the desk. Standing to extinguish the single lamp, the figure moved with the fluid grace of someone accustomed to operating in shadows.

In the last sliver of light before darkness claimed the room, a distinctive ring gleamed on one finger—a platinum band set with a black stone.

The light went out, leaving only questions in the darkness.

Keep reading for a sneak peek at the
next book in Heather Slade's
Protectors Undercover Team
One Series,
Undercover Shadow

**He'll track her to
the ends of the earth to bring her home.
She's playing a deadly game
that could destroy them both.
Their love might be the only truth
in a world of lies.**

TAG

I've always trusted my instincts in the field, but Nightingale's disappearance has left me grasping at shadows. The others think I'm obsessed, but they don't understand what she means to me. Now I'm following her trail across Eastern Europe, determined to discover the truth. Was she taken against her will, or has she been working against us all along? I don't care what secrets she's keeping—I'll find her and bring her back, because a life without Leila is unthinkable.

NIGHTINGALE

They think they know me, but no one sees the real me—not even Tag. My disappearance wasn't an accident—it was my only choice after what I discovered in Syria. Now I'm moving east with handlers always watching, playing a dangerous game where one wrong move means death. The tunnels beneath the Highland estates hold secrets that could bring down governments. As Tag gets closer, I'm terrified he'll become collateral damage in a war he doesn't even know exists. But if anyone can navigate this labyrinth and survive, it's the man I never meant to love.

1

Nightingale

I stared out at the London sky, finding no stars tonight, only darkness broken by the city's endless lights. From my safe house window in Notting Hill, I tracked the shadows moving across the wet pavement below, mentally cataloging each suspicious figure. My breath created small patches of fog on the cold glass, temporary markers of my existence that disappeared seconds later.

They were following me again tonight. Different faces, same purpose. They weren't even trying to be subtle anymore.

My mobile vibrated—the third burner this week. The text contained only coordinates and a time—zero two hundred. Thirty minutes from now. Another move, another location, another step in this elaborate game where I still couldn't identify all the players.

My gaze drifted to the small tracking device I'd extracted from my tactical vest after Syria. I'd disabled it immediately, of course, but hadn't destroyed it. Sentimental, perhaps. Or something deeper.

Tag would have found me by now if I'd left it active.

The thought of him sent a familiar ache through my chest. I could almost see him pacing his study at Glenshadow, his dark eyes intense as he tracked intelligence feeds, searching for any trace of me. Niall MacTaggert didn't surrender, didn't abandon his people. Especially not someone he'd shared his bed with.

What would he think of me now?

I turned away from the window, methodically packing the few possessions I was able to bring with me. Everything fit into a single backpack—the mark of an operative who knew better than to grow attached to physical things.

Or people.

My fingers paused on a faded photograph, its edges worn from frequent handling. Four figures stood before a Highland backdrop—Tag, Con, Ash, and Gus. I'd taken it during a rare moment of celebration after a successful mission. Before Fallon Wallace. Before Labyrinth. Before I discovered the truth buried in the encrypted files in Damascus.

"You shouldn't keep that," a woman's voice said from the doorway.

I didn't startle. I'd known she was there before she spoke—the subtle shift in the air pressure, the nearly imperceptible creak of the floorboard.

"Sentimentality is a liability," she continued, remaining in the shadows. "Especially for someone in your position."

"My position being what, exactly?" I slipped the photo into my jacket pocket. "Prisoner? Asset? Double agent?"

A soft laugh escaped her lips. "Let's call it…consultant. Your expertise regarding Sterling's neural interface research is invaluable to our continued work."

"And what about Tag?" I asked, keeping my voice neutral. "He won't stop looking."

"The Earl of Glenshadow is persistent, I grant you." The woman shifted slightly, still concealing her face. "But he's following the breadcrumbs we've carefully placed. By the time he realizes the truth, it will be too late."

I turned back to the window, hiding my expression. "You underestimate him."

"Perhaps." She sounded amused. "Or perhaps you overestimate his feelings for you. Men like MacTaggert love the chase more than the capture."

I didn't respond to the barb. Let her believe what she wanted about my relationship with Tag. The less she understood, the better.

"Our contact will arrive soon. Be ready." She paused at the doorway. "And, Agent Nassar? Do remember where your loyalties lie now."

When her footsteps faded, I extracted a small tool from my boot heel and pried up a floorboard beneath the bed. Inside the shallow space lay a tactical communications device—not standard Unit 23 issue, but something more specialized.

I activated it and composed a message in the unique encryption protocol only three people in the world could decrypt. My warning needed to be clear without revealing too much.

Janus active. McLaren remains in play. Tunnels vital.

I hesitated, thumb hovering over the send button, hating what I'd sacrificed to infiltrate what remained of Labyrinth.

But Tag needed to know I hadn't betrayed him.

After a moment's hesitation, I added a final line:

Trust in Loch Fyne. Everything else is shadow.

The reference would mean nothing to anyone else—just a geographical location in Scotland. But Tag would remember the night we'd spent together on his boat, anchored in the sheltered waters of the loch. The things we'd whispered in the darkness. The promises made.

I sent the message, then immediately disassembled the device, scattering its components in different locations around the room—the heating vent, the toilet tank, the hollow curtain rod. Nothing recognizable would remain when they searched the place after my departure.

Outside, a car engine started. Across the street, a figure stepped from the shadows, eyes tilted upward toward my window.

I recognized the silhouette immediately, my heart freezing in my chest.

Tag.

He'd found me, despite everything.

But he couldn't approach—not with them watching. Not with what I still needed to accomplish.

I stepped back from the window, out of sight, my decision made before I fully processed my options. Retrieving the burner phone, I typed quickly:

ABORT. COMPROMISED. MOVING EAST.

Then I gathered my backpack, checked my weapon, and slipped into the hallway.

By the time Tag breached the safe house, I would be gone.

Again.

About the Author

USA Today best-selling author Heather Slade writes shamelessly sexy, edge-of-your seat romantic suspense.

She gave herself the gift of writing a book for her own birthday one year. Sixty-plus books later (and counting), she's having the time of her life.

The women Slade writes are self-confident, strong, with wills of their own, and hearts as big as the Colorado sky. The men are sublimely sexy, seductive alphas who rise to the challenge of capturing the sweet soul of a woman whose heart they'll hold in the palm of their hand forever. Add in a couple of neck-snapping twists and turns, a page-turning mystery, and a swoon-worthy HEA, and you'll be holding one of her books in your hands.

She loves to hear from her readers. You can contact her at heather@heatherslade.com

To keep up with her latest news and releases, please visit her website at www.heatherslade.com to sign up for her newsletter.

MORE FROM AUTHOR HEATHER SLADE

BUTLER RANCH
Kade's Worth
Brodie's Promise
Maddox's Truce
Naughton's Secret
Mercer's Vow
Kade's Return
Butler Ranch Christmas

WICKED WINEMAKERS
FIRST LABEL
Brix's Bid
Ridge's Release
Press' Passion
Zin's Sins
Tryst's Temptation

WICKED WINEMAKERS
SECOND LABEL
Beau's Beloved
Cru's Crush
Bit's Bliss
Snapper's Seduction
Kick's Kiss

ROARING FORK RANCH
Roaring Fork Wrangler
Roaring Fork Roughstock
Roaring Fork Rockstar
Roaring Fork Rooker
Roaring Fork Bridger

PROTECTORS
UNDERCOVER TEAM ONE
Undercover Agent
Undercover Emissary
Undercover Savior
Undercover Infidel
Undercover Shadow

PROTECTORS
UNDERCOVER TEAM TWO
Undercover Renegade
Undercover Archon
Undercover Rogue
Undercover Vanguard
Undercover Paragon

K19 GENESIS COALITION
Code Name: Sundance
Code Name: Rawhide
Code Name: Dallas
Code Name: Wraith
Code Name: Preacher

K19 SECURITY
SOLUTIONS TEAM ONE
Razor's Edge
Gunner's Redemption
Mistletoe's Magic
Mantis' Desire
Dutch's Salvation

K19 SECURITY
SOLUTIONS TEAM TWO
Striker's Choice
Monk's Fire
Halo's Oath
Tackle's Honor
Onyx's Awakening

K19 SHADOW OPERATIONS
TEAM ONE
Code Name: Ranger
Code Name: Diesel
Code Name: Wasp
Code Name: Cowboy
Code Name: Mayhem

K19 ALLIED INTELLIGENCE
TEAM ONE
Code Name: Ares
Code Name: Cayman
Code Name: Poseidon
Code Name: Zeppelin
Code Name: Magnet

K19 ALLIED INTELLIGENCE
TEAM TWO
Code Name: Puck
Code Name: Michelangelo
Code Name: Typhon
Code Name: Hornet
Code Name: Reaper

New series coming soon:
MINERVA PROTOCOL
Code Name: Blackjack
Code Name: Dagger
Code Name: Nexus
Code Name: Ember
Code Name: Nomad

K19 SENTINEL CYBER
TEAM ONE
Code Name: Admiral
Code Name: Dante
Code Name: Grit
Code Name: Tank
Code Name: Atticus

K19 SENTINEL CYBER
TEAM TWO
Code Name: Admiral
Code Name: Dante
Code Name: Grit
Code Name: Tank
Code Name: Atticus

THE ROYAL AGENTS
OF MI6
Make Me Shiver
Drive Me Wilder
Feel My Pinch
Chase My Shadow
Find My Angel

THE INVINCIBLES
TEAM ONE
Code Name: Deck
Code Name: Edge
Code Name: Grinder
Code Name: Rile
Code Name: Smoke

THE INVINCIBLES
TEAM TWO
Code Name: Buck
Code Name: Irish
Code Name: Saint
Code Name: Hammer
Code Name: Rip

THE UNSTOPPABLES
TEAM ONE
Code Name: Fury
Code Name: Merried
Code Name: Vex
Code Name: Steel
Code Name: Jagger

COWBOYS OF
CRESTED BUTTE
A Cowboy Falls
A Cowboy's Dance
A Cowboy's Kiss
A Cowboy Stays
A Cowboy Wins